www.alohalagoonmysteries.com

ALOHA LAGOON MYSTERIES

Ukulele Murder
Murder on the Aloha Express
Deadly Wipeout
Deadly Bubbles in the Wine
Mele Kalikimaka Murder
Death of the Big Kahuna
Ukulele Deadly
Bikinis & Bloodshed
Death of the Kona Man
Lethal Tide
Beachboy Murder
Handbags & Homicide
Tiaras & Terror
Photo Finished
Fatal Break
Death Under the Sea
Tidal Wave
Death on a Cliff
Hula Homicide
Hallo-waiian Murder Mystery

HALLO-WAIIAN MURDER MYSTERY

---

an Aloha Lagoon mystery

Rosalie Spielman

Eric
Thank you
for your support.
Rosalie
Spielman

HALLO-WAIIAN MURDER MYSTERY

Published by Gemma Halliday Publishing

Thank you to my family and friends for their continued love and support. Thank you to my agent, Dawn Dowdle, for her continued faith in me. And thank you to my editor and publisher for rolling with the surprise Halloween book I handed in.

Mahalo!
Rosalie Spielman

CHAPTER ONE

"Kiki Hepburn, are you *trying* to kill me?!" Oliana Harris growled, jabbing a gnarly index finger at me. Then she turned her finger toward the table and pointed at the small mountain of Halloween-themed candy piled in the center. She glared at me again.

"No, of course not, Mrs. Harris." I plucked a hard candy from the pile and held it up. "See, some are sugar-free." Halloween was in a few days, and despite the mildly tropical weather, we were trying to get into the spirit.

Auntie Akamai appeared at my side with a platter of tiny mummy-dogs, celery sticks made into witches' brooms, and amputated finger shortbread cookie-sticks. She gave me a sly smile and a shake of her head before turning to her friend. "Kiki did exactly as I told her, and *I* would never try to kill you."

"I might," muttered Celine from the couch behind us.

"No one is killing anyone," said Margaux as she came out from the kitchen and expertly lowered a tray of drinks. She served the drinks to the places their owners would sit, announcing the Halloweeny nicknames she gave the drinks as she handed them out. Then she clapped her hands and picked up her own drink. "Let's have a toast!"

The four older ladies, now all smiles, went to stand behind their chairs and lifted their drinks. In unison, they chanted, "*Friends through thin, friends through thick, let's play mahjong and drink 'til we're sick!*"

I hid my shock behind my Ghoul-arita but joined them in the following laughter and clinking of glasses. Auntie Akamai turned to me to toast her wineglass against mine and gave me a wink.

The ladies took small plates of appetizers to their places around the card table, while I perched on a stool from the kitchen. It was Auntie Akamai's turn to host this week, as she usually did the first Tuesday of the month. I was there to watch and learn how to play mahjong.

Until I moved to Aloha Lagoon and in with Auntie Akamai, I thought mahjong was a relaxing electronic matching game and was confused why Auntie Akamai and her friends gathered once a week to play. From what I observed so far, it didn't resemble the computer game at all.

All the tiles—which looked like pieces of mozzarella cheese—were scrambled face down in the center of the table, and each woman drew seventeen tiles and laid them in front of themselves stacked two high, with the remaining tiles building a "wall" around the inside of the table. The women then took turns putting a tile into the center of the table and drawing a tile from the wall. The goal wasn't to match identical tiles, like the computer version, but rather make sets in the racks in front of each player.

Since Auntie Akamai was hosting, she would be the dealer, so the person to her right played first. That was Oliana Harris, an adorable older lady with the temperament of Chuckie, the demon doll. Her hair was as tightly permed as she was wound, which was certainly not good for her multitude of health conditions. Diabetes was one of those, which she constantly reminded everyone. Irrelevant to her health, she was also filthy rich, a pineapple heiress.

Not that there was anything wrong with being an heiress; I was one too, my father being a real estate developer headquartered in New York City. I hoped by getting away from that life I wouldn't turn out shallow and aimless, but after meeting Oliana, I also hoped I wouldn't become a nasty old lady.

Next to Oliana was Celine Suzuki, a former teacher. She was as sweet as pie, not a dramatic bone in her petite fit and trim body. Her hair was the most beautiful gray I had ever seen, long and silver, and her dark eyes sparkled mischievously. I wondered, not for the first time, if the woman was actually a fairy.

Rounding out the "squad" was Margaux LaRoux, a former bartender with a trace of a Louisiana accent. She was definitely the most laid-back of the group, the most into the Island Time way of life, which was ironic since she wasn't born and raised here like the others. Originally from outside of New Orleans, she wasn't any younger than the other ladies, but she hid it better. She wore her hair natural in an Afro, humidity be damned, and wore faded, stylishly torn jeans and a sleeveless flowered blouse which showcased her yoga-toned arms.

I had heard about these three other women ever since I met Auntie Akamai. She referred to them as her "widow squad," since all four had lost their husbands rather young. Auntie Akamai wore her usual flowery muumuu-style dress and her ever-present smile. Usually, I made myself scarce when it was Auntie Akamai's week to host. But with no sunset dive to lead at the dive shop, I had no work. And Dex had a cold, so no date with my handsome Hawaiian hunk either.

So instead, I perched on a stool between Auntie Akamai and Margaux, watching them play and listening to their playful banter. We were joined by Paulie, Auntie Akamai's Amazon gray parrot, who flew over and landed on my shoulder. He wasn't allowed closer to the table, as he was known to make away with mahjong tiles. Apparently, he liked the ones that looked vaguely like squashed bugs.

I had warmed up to Paulie considerably these last few months, especially after moving into Auntie Akamai's bungalow guest room from the detached screened in porch in the yard, which she euphemistically called her "furnished lanai." I wasn't sure Paulie had warmed up to me though, as he had taken to screaming "ding dong!" every time he saw me. At first I thought he was being a doorbell, announcing my presence to Auntie Akamai, but eventually realized he was *calling me* a ding dong. I realized this after hearing him make the actual doorbell noise for the doorbell.

Not that anyone used Auntie Akamai's doorbell. Most just opened the door and shouted a hello. Case in point, the food delivery guy who arrived shortly after we sat down. He simply rapped his knuckles on the doorframe and stuck his head in.

"Delivery!" the dark-haired teenager called to us.

"Come on in, Noah," said Auntie Akamai, waving a hand to the young Hawaiian man.

Noah shouldered the door open and made his way over, lugging two food delivery bags.

Celine hopped up and took a bag from him. She set it on the table and began digging out the food containers. Noah did the same with the remaining bag.

"You're lookin' good, Noah!" Margaux said to him. "Love the hair."

"It's hideous," spat Oliana, giving her tight perm a disgusted shake. "A mullet? Wasn't attractive in the 80s, and it's not attractive now."

"Thanks, Grandmother," Noah said flatly.

"Oh, Oliana, all the young men are wearing that style now," said Celine. "It's so his lovely curls show out the back of his helmet and you can still tell it's him. Isn't that right, Noah?"

"What do you play?" I asked him.

Noah turned pink. "Football," he said.

"I like your hair," I said. "It's stylish, and it's cute." I shot a look at Oliana.

Noah flushed scarlet. "Thanks," he muttered.

"I like it too," added Auntie Akamai. "Not that I count for anything."

He bobbed his head and scurried away, the wooden doorframe smacking behind him.

"He didn't even wait for a tip!" Auntie Akamai laughed. "Next time I want to skip a tip, I know who to call!" She reached over and patted my knee. "Would you mind grabbing the chopsticks from the kitchen?"

I nodded and carefully hopped off my stool before trotting to the kitchen, my shoulder decoration chanting "Chop-stick, chop-stick, chop-stick" as I walked. I snagged a bamboo canister from the counter and brought it out, setting it on the table by Auntie Akamai's elbow.

Celine held out a food container to me. "This must be yours, sweetheart, as it's not anyone else's normal order."

"Thank you, Miss Celine." I took my container of lo mein and grabbed a pair of chopsticks then climbed back on my stool. Paulie tipped his head to look into my container and pronounced it to be "worms."

Thanks, Paulie.

The women dug into their food, bantering back and forth, sharing bites of their food, and taking turns picking up and laying down mahjong tiles on the table in front of them, and shuffling them around on their racks.

I took my phone from my back pocket and scrolled through my social media feed, liking anything remotely fall-related. I hadn't experienced fall here in Aloha Lagoon yet and, for the first time, found myself feeling homesick. Or maybe leaf-sick, as I loved fall in New York and New England in general, the turning leaves, the crisp air… My parents took every opportunity to send pictures of the trees turning, probably in an attempt to lure me home.

Auntie Akamai's voice cut into my thoughts, her tone catching my attention due to its urgency. I glanced up.

Auntie Akamai was leaning forward, her eyes fixed on Celine. "Are you okay, C?" she asked.

I could see why she was concerned. Celine had a hand to her forehead, and when she pulled it away, I could see she was ghostly pale and sweating.

"You know, I'm not feeling very good," Celine said. She pulled at the already-loose neckline of her lightweight cowl neck sweater.

Conversation stopped, and everyone focused on her. Margaux reached out a hand to her arm.

"I think I need..." Celine stood then swayed.

"Whoa," said Margaux. She stood and grabbed Celine's arm with her other hand as well. "I think you should sit."

But instead of sitting, Celine keeled over and hit the floor with a sickening thud, her beautiful, long silver hair fanned out around her head.

CHAPTER TWO

An hour later, I sat on the couch next to Auntie Akamai, holding the older woman's hand tightly in mine. Margaux sat on her other side, and Oliana sat on a chair. We had been sitting in stunned silence.

"Akamai, I cannot believe you have not upgraded your living room set," Oliana said, shifting her body like she was sitting on a cement bench. The bamboo furniture with its palm frond print material, straight out of the show *The Golden Girls*, was overly comfortable, if anything.

Auntie Akamai raised her head and stared at her. "Really?" she asked incredulously. "Our friend since elementary school just collapsed and was taken away by an ambulance, and that is what you are concerned about?"

Oliana raised a hand and gave Auntie Akamai's words a shooing wave off. "Oh, she'll be fine. She was having an allergic reaction."

Margaux sighed. "Yes, and we dealt with it, but that doesn't mean we should be insulting our friend's furniture, Oliana."

I glanced at Oliana to see her reaction. After watching the women interact this evening, it was immediately clear that both Celine and Akamai deferred to Oliana; Celine out of fear of her wrath, and Akamai because she didn't have time for her friend's attitude. I had listened to Auntie Akamai rant about her friend on several occasions over the past nine months.

Margaux on the other hand, had a lot of experience dealing with belligerent bar customers and had no trouble handling Oliana and her often cranky behavior. Her words had the intended effect on the irritated old woman.

Oliana sighed. "I'm sorry, Akamai. I'm just worried about Celine."

Auntie Akamai nodded. "Me too." She looked at me and squeezed my hand. "Thank goodness Kiki here is up to date on CPR."

I ducked my head. "We had to get certified for work. I hope I did it right."

Honestly though, a video on social media that said to do CPR compressions to the beat of the Bee Gees "Staying Alive" stuck with me more than the class had, but I didn't think I should mention that. Margaux had given me a strange look when she heard me singing under my breath but hadn't said anything.

I looked at Margaux. "I didn't know anything about EpiPens though."

Margaux had been the one who'd recognized the signs of an allergic reaction and had administered the EpiPen Celine carried in her purse.

Auntie Akamai shook her head. "I don't understand how shellfish got into her food though. We always are very clear, and the restaurant certainly knows by now." She turned to me. "We've been ordering from them forever. The chef is Oliana's son."

Oliana muttered something under her breath that I didn't catch—but it didn't sound like a compliment.

"What about the other food?" I said, hoping to get Oliana's son off the hook, even though I had never met him.

"We made the appetizers. I know I didn't add anything shellfish related. I know better," said Auntie Akamai.

"And I made the drinks," added Margaux. "Not many drinks include shellfish."

"Did anyone's food include shellfish?" I asked, looking around at the other women.

They all shook their heads.

"What was your meal?" Margaux asked me. "I know Paulie called it *worms*, but I assume it wasn't."

I grimaced as I shook my head. "Chicken lo mein. No shrimp."

We fell silent for a few minutes until Paulie, on the back of a chair at the table, screeched "Worms!"

We all laughed, and then Auntie Akamai let go of my hand and stood. "We should probably clean up."

Auntie Akamai went to the kitchen for a trash bag while Margaux and I started gathering up the detritus of the short-lived party. When she returned with the bag, we started dropping the takeout containers into it. Aunt Akamai gathered up her chopsticks and took them and their container back to the kitchen.

I leaned closer to Margaux. "Do you think we should save her food for testing?"

She pursed her lips and paused for a moment. Then she shook her head. "No, I'm sure it's just an accident and she's okay. No harm, no foul."

Just a little *fowl*.

I nodded and dumped Celine's container into the trash bag. Once it was full, I took it to the outside garbage can at the back of the house. When I got back, Margaux was in the kitchen loading her flat-bottomed tote bag with most of the bottles of alcohol. Auntie Akamai only kept the occasional bottle of wine and a rarely touched bottle of Crown Royale.

I waited with her, and then together we walked to the living room, where Auntie Akamai was finished boxing up the mahjong set, which she handed to Oliana before wiping down the card table. Oliana was still sitting in the chair.

"I guess that chair is more comfortable now?" I said sweetly.

Oliana must not have heard me, as she had no reaction. Her perma-frown was focused on the flowers on the coffee table. Celine had brought them to the gathering.

Auntie Akamai tutted at me before returning to the kitchen. I swore I saw a hint of a smile.

Margaux and I folded up the table, and I leaned it against the back of Oliana's chair.

Paulie flapped away when I began folding the chairs, landing on the back of Auntie Akamai's usual TV-watching chair.

Which happened to be the same chair Oliana was sitting in.

"Ew, come on, you stinky chicken!" Oliana grunted, shifting to sit forward in the chair. She turned halfway so she could glare at Paulie. "Stinky chicken," she repeated.

"Stinky chicken," Paulie replied in her voice, tipping his head to eyeball her sidewise.

"Now I know where Paulie picked that up from," I said to Margaux.

She smiled. "He's on particularly good behavior tonight. He usually fights with her all night."

"He's probably scared," I said, folding the last chair and stacking it with the others against the wall. "He reads Auntie Akamai and responds to her behavior." I turned and looked toward the kitchen again. "I should probably check on her."

She met me in the doorway as she was returning to the living room. She was holding her cell phone and staring at it as she walked right past me as if I wasn't even there.

I stared after her. "Auntie Akamai? Everything okay?"

She sank onto the couch, shaking her head. "No. No," she said.

Margaux and I took the spots next to her where we were before, and Oliana finally stopped staring at the flowers.

"What is it, Akamai?" she said, her regular growl an octave higher than usual.

"I called Celine's son to see how she was doing. He's still at the hospital," she said, still staring at the phone.

When she didn't continue, Oliana leaned forward, repeating, "What is it, Akamai?"

"She's dead," Auntie Akamai whispered.

"What?!" said Oliana.

"I said she's dead!" Auntie Akamai shouted.

I leaned back, surprised. I had never heard her yell before.

"I heard what you said," Oliana said quietly. "I was expressing shock."

"But…how?" asked Margaux. "I thought it was an allergic reaction? I thought she would be fine!"

I had had my doubts but hadn't voiced them before. Celine's condition seemed much worse than a simple allergic reaction.

"Was it a heart attack?" I asked Auntie Akamai.

She nodded. "Heart attack." A sob escaped.

Oliana moaned and sat back. "I'm the one with the bad heart, but she has a heart attack? That makes no sense." She covered her face with a hand. "It should have been me."

* * *

The next morning I had to be up early for a dive. I got up extra early, intending to make the lunches and let Auntie Akamai sleep in, but she was already up, frying up Spam, slices of white bread spread out in pairs on the counter already coated in mayonnaise.

I went over and gave her a kiss on the cheek. "I can take care of this, Auntie," I said. "You can get more sleep."

Auntie Akamai snorted. "Sleep? You're assuming I had any to begin with."

I turned away to get the giant box of small chip bags out of the pantry.

"I'm sorry, Kiki. That was sweet of you to offer," Auntie Akamai said when I turned back around. "I wasn't sleeping. I kept replaying everything in my mind."

I gave her a sad smile and rubbed her shoulder. "I imagine you were. I know this is hard for you."

She nodded and sniffled, turning away to the pan of Spam spitting away on the stove. I noted the uncharacteristic slump of her shoulders and watched them rise with a sigh. She flipped all the slices before saying anything further.

"Other than her allergy, she was healthier than all of us. I just don't understand how this happened," Auntie Akamai said, shaking her head.

I had no idea what to say. I hopped onto a stool and set to braiding my long brunette hair instead. All my blonde highlights had grown out or faded enough that they looked like natural highlights. By the time I was done, she had removed the Spam slices and laid them out to cool and turned her attention to putting the chips and napkins into the crate I used to carry the lunches in.

There was a light knock on the door out on the back lanai, and Dex appeared a moment later. He went straight to Auntie Akamai and gave her a hug.

"I'm so sorry to hear about Miss Celine," he said, patting her back.

She held him in the hug longer than usual then pushed her way out of it, wiping at her eyes.

"Thank you, *keiki*," Auntie Akamai said to him, using the Hawaiian for nephew, as she patted his cheek. "I appreciate it."

"She was a nice lady and a good teacher," Dex said. After a few more moments, he turned to me.

I hopped down from the stool and into his arms for a hug. I tipped my head up for a kiss, but he reared back.

"I'm still a little stuffy," he said, pointing at his nose. "I don't want to get you sick."

I pretended to pout a little but kissed my finger then bopped him on the nose. "There."

Dex smiled that sexy smile and winked.

"So you're on boat duty today, then, Dex?" asked Auntie Akamai.

"Oh, yeah. I'm not diving with my head feeling like this," he said. "It's all Kiki today, though Dad will go down too since there's enough for two groups."

We stood, hand in hand, watching Auntie Akamai assemble the sandwiches, and then I helped her wrap them and put them in the crate. When we were done, Dex hefted up the crate, and I followed him out to the car.

CHAPTER THREE

A few hours later, I came up after the first dive of the day. We would rest and eat lunch before going down again. I was amused to see Dex snoring on a bench, but his father—and our boss—Kahiau, was less than amused.

"What if we had had an emergency while you're up here catching some Zs?" Kahiau said to Dex quietly, off to the side. "Not only could someone have been seriously hurt, but we would have gotten sued!"

Dex stood with his head hanging. "I know, I'm sorry. I didn't mean to. I'm still tired."

"Well, next time stay home if you're too tired," Kahiau said, and he turned back to the clients. His face cleared and he pasted on his big smile as he turned, and the divers had no idea there had been any issue.

I had been returning tanks to the rack and now shuffled away to keep helping the divers get out of their equipment. I was not going to say anything, mostly because I agreed completely with Kahiau. It was funny, yet not.

"Did your group see anything out of the ordinary, Kiki?" Kahiau asked me as he lugged a tank past me.

"No *honu* today, unfortunately," I said. I loved seeing the Hawaiian green sea turtles but hadn't spied one of the protected creatures today. And it was a relief. While most divers were appropriately respectful of the sea life, there could be overly enthusiastic clients who wanted a perfect picture.

"We saw a manta ray," said one woman from Kahiau's group.

"Oh, that's cool!" I said to her before Kahiau caught my eye and gave a small shake of his head with a smile. *Oh*. She just *thought* she saw one.

I passed around lunches and answered questions about sea life as Kahiau had introduced me as the "resident marine biologist." I waved it off every time, as having a degree in marine biology does not a biologist make. Having said that, I could answer most questions, but usually due to my experiences underwater here in Kauai.

Dex stayed at the other end of the boat, limiting exposure to the group or perhaps sulking.

After the clients finished eating, most of them basked in the sun. I was surprised there were as many visitors as there were, being a few days before Halloween. It seemed like an odd time of year to travel. The entire group seemed to know each other, so I asked one of the women what brought them to Hawaii. I had assumed it was for a family reunion or something, but turned out it was a destination wedding group.

"A Halloween-themed Hawaiian wedding!" the woman exclaimed. "A Hallo-wedding! We just couldn't choose between the two, so we decided, what the heck, let's combine the two!"

I must've frowned in response, though I didn't mean to. "So will you have bloody pineapples or something?"

"Yes!" the woman—apparently the bride-to-be—exclaimed. "I mean, it will be like cherry syrup, but yeah, the décor will have bloody pineapples with knives sticking out of them, and my dress is like a zombie dress. My groom's outfit is a zombie-Hawaiian shirt."

"Wow," I said. "I've never heard of anything like that before. That's certainly original!"

The bride-to-be grabbed my hand. "You should totally come! Will you?"

I had gotten the spontaneous invites before but usually demurred, telling them I didn't want to interfere with their big day. Which was funny really, since when people I actually knew and had been friends with came to get married, no one in that group had said anything about me coming to the wedding. Not that I'd really wanted to anyway, especially after one of their party tried to kill me.

But this themed wedding was just too interesting to pass up. And I didn't have any plans for Halloween anyway.

"If you're sure, I'd love to," I said, smiling.

"Great!" the woman said. "I'm Shannon. That's Tim, my fiancé, over there." She pointed to the other side of the boat, where a man who was looking like he was edging into the territory of a sunburn was sitting.

"Oh! Gosh, Tim, you're getting burnt!" Shannon jumped up and trotted over to him with a bottle of sunscreen. She gazed adoringly at her fiancé.

"It's okay, babe. A peeling sunburn will add to the grossness of a zombie," Tim laughed.

Ew. But he wasn't wrong.

I headed to the other end of the boat to tell Dex about my new Halloween plans and to see if he'd want to be my plus one.

"That sounds weird," he muttered. "But also pretty awesome." He smiled up at me. "It's a date."

* * *

I spent most of the second dive letting the silence of the underwater world ease my stress. It was what I loved about diving—the silence, the peace. It was an excellent time to think.

Unfortunately, today that thinking time was spent going over the previous evening to see if I could recognize any signs of illness in Celine. The only thing that stood out was that some of the women had shared bites of their food—could one of them have had shellfish in theirs?

I pointed out some clownfish nestled in the wriggling arms of sea anemone, always a fan favorite ever since *Finding Nemo*, according to Kahiau. Next, I led the group to some banded coral shrimp, their bright red and white stripes almost blending in with the coral. I hovered behind the other divers as they swam in for a closer look.

Those shrimps got me wondering though. What exactly did a shellfish allergy include? Was it only clams and oysters, or did it include shrimp and crab, what we would usually refer to as crustaceans? I would have to do an internet search when I was back on dry land.

When time was up and air was getting low, I gave the ascend hand signal to the group and we headed for the surface.

Dex reached a hand down to help haul me out of the water. "A pod of dolphins came by," he said. "It would be excellent if they came back."

He helped me out of my BCD, or Buoyancy Control Device—the vest that the air tank was connected to and allowed me to descend and ascend—and I in turn helped the clients up the last rung of the ladder.

I kept an eye out for the dolphins as I helped Kahiau's group onboard and as we prepared the boat for our return to shore. Finally, as we were heading in, the pod made its appearance, jumping in and out of the wake of our boat. The playful creatures were, as always, a hit with both the tourists and us residents alike.

Back at the dive shop after we unloaded, Shannon, the Halloween bride, asked for my contact information so she could send me the wedding details.

"I'm excited about this," I said, tapping my info into the contacts of her phone. "It sounds like fun!"

"I hope so!" Shannon laughed nervously. "Our Hallo-wedding will either be really cool or super cheesy."

"It's Halloween," I said, handing her phone back. "Things are allowed to be crazy on that night, you know?"

Shannon grinned at me. "That's what we are banking on." She gave me a wave and ran off to join her party as they headed back to the Aloha Lagoon Resort on foot. "See you then!"

* * *

I bounded up the steps into the house to tell Auntie Akamai the news about the Hallo-wedding. After I burst through the door and found Auntie Akamai sitting on her couch with a box of tissues, my bubble burst into a million guilty little pieces. I sat on the couch next to her and pondered what to say.

Auntie Akamai looked at me. "I have to go offer condolences to Celine's family. Will you come with me?"

I reached a hand across to pat hers. "Of course, Auntie. What time do you want to go?"

A half hour later, we were in her car, a covered dish on her lap and me at the wheel. After six months, Auntie Akamai put her foot down and said it was time for me to learn how to drive, saying if I didn't get my license, she would charge me for her taxi service. So, I had gotten my permit and was practicing my driving regularly.

It had started pouring, and I hadn't driven in such heavy rain before, so we'd be lucky if we got to Celine's house in the next hour, even though it was only six miles away.

Auntie Akamai didn't say a word, other than to tell me when and where to turn. She had taught her own children how to drive and was probably the calmest woman I had ever met.

Finally, we pulled up in front of a small bungalow-style house. There were already several cars there, so I would need to park farther away, but since it was raining, I let Auntie Akamai out in front of the house.

"Don't crash my car," she said before dashing off for the house.

I parked down a few houses where there were no other cars—parallel parking was still a mystery to me—and hurried back down the sidewalk. Auntie Akamai had waited on the porch for me, which I appreciated. I noted the plethora of plants in Celine's yard, which made a virtual forest of flowers. If the weather had been nicer, it would be a lovely place to linger.

After a quick knock, the door swung open to a puffy-eyed young woman who looked to be about my age and seemed vaguely familiar. She was dressed in a loose and light though long-sleeved black sweater over a black miniskirt.

"Oh, Auntie, thank you for coming," she said, and pulled Auntie Akamai into the house.

They hugged, and then Auntie Akamai turned to me. "This is Kiki, my friend and roommate," she said to the woman. "Kiki, this is Analise, Celine's niece. I think you two are about the same age."

Analise eyed me. "I recognize you from around. You're dating Dex, right?" She had gorgeous long black hair and an enviable figure, so I imagined Dex knew exactly who she was.

I blushed. "Yes. Nice to meet you. I'm sorry about your aunt."

Analise nodded, tears springing to her eyes. "Thank you." She stepped back so we could enter farther and she could close the door against the steady rain then reached for Auntie Akamai's covered dish. "I'll put this on the table."

The front room was full of people, some holding small plates or cups, chatting to others, while a few sat on the couch or chairs and stared into space. One very old-looking woman sat in the middle of everyone and everything, like she was holding court. Auntie Akamai headed directly for her. She bent over and took the old woman's hand, speaking quietly to her.

"That's my grandma," Analise said. "Isn't it horrible that her daughter died before her? She's so sad about that. Keeps saying she was supposed to go first."

I could see the resemblance between Celine and the old woman, so I nodded. Another woman who also looked like Celine was across the room. She looked roughly the same age as Celine too, but her hair only had strands of silver instead of being completely silver like her sister's.

"Is that your mother?" I asked her, nodding with my chin.

Analise looked surprised but nodded. "And my dad next to her, and those two men are my cousins, Aunt Celine's sons." She pointed at two men standing behind Analise's grandmother. They looked to be in their thirties, so Celine must have been the older sister by a decent amount. Analise continued, "There's another son who lives in Colorado. He's on his way home but not here yet."

Analise's mom seemed to sense she was being spoken about and looked over at us. After a moment, she started over to us.

"You must be Kiki, the one who did CPR on my sister?" she asked.

"Yes, I tried," I said.

"Thank you for trying," Analise's mother said. "I know it didn't help in the end, but that's not your fault, of course." She turned to her daughter and reached for the covered dish. "I'll deliver that," she said.

There was a new knock on the door behind me, so I moved away from it. Analise opened it to a young man standing there, drenched and shivering from the rain. It took me a moment, since seeing him here was out of context, but it was the teenager who'd delivered food the night of the game.

"Noah," said Analise. "Come on in."

Noah shook his head, making droplets fall. "I don't want to get your floor wet."

"It's okay," Analise said, reaching for his arm. "Everyone else has dripped on it too."

Noah took a few steps into the house, his wide eyes darting around. He continued to shake so much that I wondered if it was more than being cold.

"Do you want a towel?" Analise asked him.

He showered us with droplets when he shook his head a second time. That mullet hairstyle was certainly a good one for holding water, especially with his curls. "I don't want to stay long. I wanted to say how sorry I was. Miss Celine was my favorite teacher. She was just the best!"

And then he burst into tears.

Analise turned to me, horrified. I stared back at her, and then we both faced Noah again.

"I'm sorry," the boy sobbed. "I'm so sorry!"

Then he turned and ran out the door, letting the screen bang behind him.

The entire room had fallen silent, staring at the scene. I wanted to melt into one of the puddles already on the floor.

"I guess he really liked Aunt Celine when she was his teacher," Analise finally said to the room.

Heads nodded, and people turned away and back to the food and conversation.

"That seemed a bit extreme, didn't it?" Analise whispered to me.

"When did he have her as a teacher?" I asked. "I mean, it must have been meaningful to him."

Analise raised her eyebrows. "My aunt taught kindergarten."

Oh.

I didn't have a response for that, so instead I told her he had delivered the food last night.

"Ah," she said. "That reaction makes a little more sense now. Maybe he's worried he caused her to have the heart attack somehow."

"Oh, that would be sad," I said. "I was wondering how you all know each other so well."

"Through my aunt and his grandma. That's how I know Dex, too, though we did go to school together too," she said. "Two years apart."

"And Noah? How far behind is he?" I asked.

"Oh, he's still in high school. He was always the little guy we all had to watch." Analise smiled. "I think he's maybe a junior, maybe a senior?" She tapped her lip. "I think he's seventeen."

"Ah," I said. "Once again I see it's a pretty tight community here."

She nodded and glanced out the door behind me. "That too." She gestured toward the back of the house. "Do you need anything to eat or drink? No one comes empty-handed to things like this. There's a ton." She gestured toward the back of the front room and lowered her voice. "I could use a shot of something myself. Especially with who is arriving now." She tipped her head to the door before turning her back to it and walking away.

I glanced over my shoulder as I followed her. A large black sedan with darkened windows had pulled up.

In the kitchen, she walked us over to a section of the counter that held a multitude of alcohol bottles. "Pick your poison," she said grimly.

CHAPTER FOUR

A couple shots each of tequila helped calm her nerves but made my judgment a little fuzzy. We did the whole salt and lime part too, which told me this was my type of gal.

"All right," I said after I blew air out between clenched teeth. "Who's car was that?"

Analise giggled, dabbing lime juice off her chin with her sleeve. "You've had the pleasure of meeting Oliana Harris, right?"

"Oh goodness. Yes."

Analise laughed at my response. Then she tiptoed over to the swinging galley door between the living room and kitchen and peeked through the crack. "I actually want to see how my grandma will react to her. She's never liked her." She glanced back at me. "I might need one more shot though. Oliana Harris drives people to drink."

As if on cue, Analise's mother came through the door, almost hitting Analise, whose reactions were still pretty quick. She looked at us clutching shot glasses and then to the bottle of tequila, saltshaker, and slices of lime. Her face held disapproval for a split second, and then she pointed.

"Pour me one."

Analise giggled then did as she was told, also refilling her own and mine while she was at it.

I handed her mother the saltshaker and set a wedge of lime in front of her. After shaking the salt onto the back of her hand, she licked it, took the shot, and then, coughing, grabbed and bit the lime wedge.

"Does that help?" Analise asked her mother.

Her mother coughed a few more times and, with eyes streaming, nodded. "It should." She glanced over at me. "I'm not much of a drinker. I'm Bette." She wiped the lime juice off her hand and held the towel to her face for a moment, patting her tears. I recognized that as a move to avoid wiping her mascara away.

After she lowered the towel, her face was unreadable. "So strange how things happen, isn't it?" Bette sighed and raised a hand in farewell. "I'd better get back out there before my mother damages Oliana Harris." She pushed her way out of the swinging door.

Analise looked at me then pointed to the tequila bottle. I nodded, and we both burst into giggles. *Yeah, I wouldn't be driving home.*

As she was pouring, I took a step closer to her. "Analise. Tell me more about your aunt Celine."

Analise frowned and set the bottle down just a smidge too hard. She handed me my shot glass. "Everyone loved her. That's the best way to describe her."

"And your uncle?" I asked. "Did people like him?" I went ahead and did the salt, followed by its companions.

Analise nodded her head. "He died a few years ago, but yes, everyone liked him. Maybe a little *too* much," she added ominously. She tipped her head. "You know what, Aunt Celine told me once my uncle dated Oliana before he dated her. Way back in high school. Isn't that crazy? The whole small world thing." She waved a dismissive hand.

"Hmm." I tapped my lip then realized my gesture was a little overdramatic. The shooters were taking effect. Big-time.

Raised voices came through the door, and we both turned toward it.

"Let's go out and watch the show," Analise said.

She pushed the swinging door, and we walked out and were greeted by what could be compared to the prelude to a WWE wrestling match. The crowd had increased, and people were shouting and struggling against arms holding them back. Noah had returned and stood in a corner, still soaking wet and sobbing.

"What the…" Analise said, and we exchanged a befuddled look.

And then I saw Auntie Akamai. She was standing in the middle of the mess, holding her hands up against the two main combatants—Oliana and Analise's grandma.

Analise shook her head, but she had a smile on her face. She lifted two fingers to her lips and let out the loudest whistle I'd ever heard.

Unfortunately for me, I was standing right next to her. My ear would be ringing for days!

Everyone turned toward her and froze, standing like stunned statues.

"Everyone, break it up. Have a little respect for Aunt Celine's memory, would you? She would be so disappointed in you." Analise looked around the room, pointing those whistle-fingers at the crowd. "*All* of you. Now, anyone who doesn't share blood with Celine Suzuki, *out*!"

I'll admit my mouth was hanging open, staring at Analise. *Dang*. She was hardcore. And someone I wanted as a friend.

But of course, this wasn't kindergarten, where you make friends by saying *I want to be your friend*, and she had just told everyone to leave.

Our eyes met, and I smiled.

Analise patted my arm. "It was nice meeting you. We should hang out sometime. But, you know, not today."

"That would be cool," I said. "I'll look you up on social media."

Analise gave me a thumbs-up then stepped away to shoo people out.

I linked arms with Auntie Akamai, and I used her to stay up on my heels. The day had turned dark and cloudy—the deluge of rain had stopped finally. Mostly stopped, at least. There was still a misty drizzle. I was accustomed to drizzle, having spent four years in Seattle. It made me a little homesick for that town.

"So," I leaned in and whispered to Auntie Akamai, "what was that all about?"

"Let's just say Celine's sister, Bette, doesn't like Oliana," Auntie Akamai said. "Nor Celine's mother. She actually blamed Oliana for Celine's death."

"What?" I stopped on the sidewalk, forcing Auntie Akamai to stop too. "How?"

"Celine's mother said Oliana was always jealous of Celine and finally 'got her way' and implied that someone in the Harris family did the work for her." Auntie Akamai shook her head. "Not appropriate, and I think perhaps she's losing her marbles a bit."

I giggled, probably not the best response. Auntie Akamai looked over at me with raised eyebrows. "Oh, I shouldn't drive, by the way." I grinned and handed over the keys.

Auntie Akamai shook her head, smiling, and went around to the other side of the car. As I was waiting for her to unlock my side, a middle-aged couple passed by arm in arm. As they did, I overheard one of them say, "Shellfish allergy, my foot. She was poisoned by that voodoo woman."

I froze and watched them walk away. Once they were out of hearing range, I got in the car. I nodded to the couple with my chin. "Who are those people?" I asked Auntie Akamai.

She glanced up from her seat belt and watched them walk away. "That's Oliana's son and daughter-in-law. Why?"

"They were saying something about Celine being poisoned by a voodoo woman. Who is the voodoo woman?" I asked. "And where the heck is that coming from?"

Auntie Akamai's face fell. "There's only one person I know who might be described as that. By prejudiced jerks, maybe."

"Who?" I repeated. *Voodoo?* Oh, no… Did they mean the only person I knew from New Orleans? "They don't mean Margaux, do they?"

Auntie Akamai nodded. "Yes, I'm afraid they do."

I stared out of the windshield after the couple. "Why would they think she poisoned Celine? Where is that even coming from?"

Aunt Akamai shook her head. "I don't have any idea, but it makes me sad."

"Okay," I said. "Tell me about them."

"Cain Harris, second child. He runs a restaurant in Aloha Lagoon, but if you ask Oliana, he's unfocused and lazy." She chuckled. "Her oldest son runs the pineapple plantation but was just diagnosed with terminal cancer. Very sad."

"Yes, that's awful," I said. Maybe that explained some of Oliana's grouchiness.

"The woman is Cain's wife, Jennifer," Auntie Akamai said. "Second wife. His first wife died years ago when Noah was younger, just a little guy."

"And what does Cain do?" I asked.

"He's the chef at his restaurant," Auntie Akamai said. "Which is the same one that delivered us the food during mahjong. His wife works there as well."

"Did she get along with Celine?" I asked.

Auntie Akamai sighed. "Everyone got along with Celine."

"Except Oliana, on occasion, right?" I asked.

"Right." Auntie Akamai sighed and looked out at the rain that had picked up again. "I have no idea why they'd suggest Celine was poisoned. Maybe they mean given the allergen that caused her reaction? But to suggest she'd been purposely poisoned?"

"Especially," I added, raising a finger sagely, "when *they* made the food."

Auntie Akamai pulled her car into her regular spot in front of the house. Neither of us were overly surprised to see a woman sitting on Auntie Akamai's porch.

"There she is, right on time," Auntie Akamai groaned as she put the car in park.

I giggled. "The gossip crow. Or is it vulture?"

Auntie Akamai's head swung to me, her eyes wide. "Kiki!" She turned the car off and picked up her bag. "She likes to…be in the know."

Chastised, I stayed quiet as I followed her toward the house.

"Stella!" Auntie Akamai said. "Isn't it just horrible?!"

Stella stood to greet us. In all honesty, Stella reminded me of a goose—short, wide, and with a nasally voice. She even had hair the color of a Canada Goose, a dull dark gray and cut into a spiky pixie cut. The only part of her hair that took away from the natural fowl look was the bright-purple tips.

"Oh, Akamai," she honked as she rushed forward, arms outstretched like she was about to take to the sky.

I covered my mouth to hold in my giggle and turned my back to gaze at the road. I squeezed my eyes shut and breathed slowly through my nose to get control of my laughter. This was bad.

Finally, I was able to turn around and follow the women into the house.

Stella was Auntie Akamai's long-time neighbor, and even though she had told me to call her auntie as well, I just never could. Mostly because her gossipy behavior, like right now, didn't inspire the warm feelings—or respect—that using the affectionate term required.

She was chattering away—not unlike geese do when they meet each other—and of course, her subject was Celine.

"Do you know what happened?" Stella asked, flapping her hands in distress. "Tell me exactly what happened!"

"She collapsed. Kiki here gave her CPR." Auntie Akamai turned to me and, unseen by Stella, gave me a stern look.

I nodded. "It wasn't enough," I said quietly.

"Oh! But sweetie, you *tried*," said Stella.

I frowned. The way she emphasized *tried* made it sound like an insult.

"What brought it on?" Stella turned back to Auntie Akamai. "Was there anything leading to it, or did she just drop like a stone?"

I stared at her. *Wow, sensitive much?*

Auntie Akamai was at a loss for words as well and simply stared at her neighbor for a long, uncomfortable moment. "I don't know, Stella." Her voice held a warning that Stella didn't pick up on.

"I mean, was it something she ate or drank, or was there an argument, something that upset her?" Stella pressed on, oblivious as always.

"I don't know, Stella," Auntie Akamai repeated more forcefully.

"But you have to know something. You were *there*. I was *not*," said Stella.

Auntie Akamai stiffened, her head rearing back. Based on that reaction, there had to be something deeper behind the comment.

I stepped up to Stella. "I think you'd better go." I took her arm and steered her toward the door.

"Excuse me!" Stella snatched her arm back. "This is not your house!" She started to turn back to Auntie Akamai.

"It is Auntie Akamai's house, yes, but I do live here," I growled. "And unlike you, I can see your incessant and thoughtless questioning is upsetting her." I placed myself in front of her, between the two women. "You need to leave."

Stella drew herself up indignantly to her full height and glared up at me. "You smell like booze," she said then turned and stomped out, slamming the door behind her.

Auntie Akamai sank into her favorite chair, and Paulie popped out from behind the couch. He made a point of disappearing when Stella came around. He was a smart bird.

"Witch," he squawked.

I had expected to be chastised for the way I spoke to Stella, but Auntie Akamai just shook her head and tutted. "You know you're going to get a reputation as the next town drunk now" was all she said.

We spent a quiet evening watching TV, though I could see Auntie Akamai wasn't paying much attention. She didn't even try at *Jeopardy*. We went to bed early.

I woke up the next morning to pouring rain, *again*. Now, it is completely possible to dive in the rain since you are underwater anyway—but on dark days it wasn't as enjoyable. Most tourists don't want to sit on a boat in the rain, and I didn't blame them one bit. I didn't want to either. And on days where there might be lightning, it was a no-go. So I wasn't surprised to have a text from Kahiau telling me the dive was canceled, but he thought this morning would be perfect for an equipment deep clean.

This was one of the few problems with my chosen career. I was an hourly worker, not salaried, so on days that we didn't do excursions, I wasn't paid. I usually made up a little time by working on the dive shop's social media accounts, but that was an hour, maybe two, at the most.

I spent a half hour working from my bed, posting an update on my social media and linking an article about Kauai sea life so divers could see some virtually since no one would be seeing it in person today.

Dex texted he'd pick me up at nine thirty, so around nine, I finally padded out of my room, my house slippers slapping on the tile floor. I found Auntie Akamai in the kitchen, staring into her Kona coffee. She didn't even look up when I came in.

I poured myself a mug of coffee and added my usual excessive amounts of both cream and sugar then joined her at the table. I looked her over and was struck by how exhausted she appeared.

"Are you doing okay?" I asked her.

Auntie Akamai sighed. "No, not really." She glanced up at me and touched her hair self-consciously. "I must look a mess."

"No," I lied. "Just a little tired, that's all."

She nodded. "Can't sleep much at the moment." She took a long sip of her coffee before setting it down and meeting my eye.

"I hear you," I said. I waited a few beats before adding that we would be cleaning at the shop today.

"All right," Auntie Akamai said, her voice flat.

I took my coffee with me to change then returned my cup to the kitchen on my way out. Auntie Akamai hadn't moved, and unless she'd refilled her cup, hadn't drunk her coffee. I set my hand on her shoulder and gave a gentle squeeze. She reached up to pat it and nodded. No words were needed.

* * *

Pulling back up to the house in Dex's Jeep after four hours of scrubbing equipment at the dive shop, we were surprised to see two cars already parked in front of Auntie Akamai's cottage.

"Who's here?" I asked Dex.

He shrugged. "I don't recognize the cars, but they're probably some friends of the mahjong group or from school."

"Oh true." I paused a moment, considering what might be going on inside. What if people were crying? "I'm not sure I want to interrupt."

"I'm sure it's okay," Dex said. "I mean, you live here. You can't be expected to not go into your home. They won't mind."

I looked over at him and smiled. "You're tired, aren't you?"

He gave me a sheepish look. "Yeah, sorry."

"It's fine. You have to be better before Halloween, so go get some rest." I patted his knee then climbed out of the Jeep. I blew Dex a kiss before heading inside.

The second I stepped through the door, I regretted it. On the couch with Auntie Akamai, holding a notebook in his hands, was Detective Ray Kahoalani.

Detective Ray was the homicide detective in Aloha Lagoon, and I had interacted with him twice before now, helping find murderers I unwittingly got involved with. And since he was a homicide detective, his presence only meant one thing.

Murder.

CHAPTER FIVE

"Come on in, Kiki," Detective Ray said. "I'll need to ask you some questions too. Do you mind waiting in the kitchen?"

I looked at Auntie Akamai's tearstained face. She gave me a nod, so I went through to the other room.

The kitchen was already occupied by two uniformed officers. One was looking through the cabinets, while the other was staring down Paulie. The parrot was sitting on the back of a kitchen chair and looked at me when I came in.

"Muuuuuurderrrrr," Paulie crooned at me.

"That is the most disturbing thing I have ever heard come out of a bird," the officer said. She glanced at me. "Is that normal behavior for him?"

I nodded. "Unfortunately."

The officer gestured at the kitchen table, so I sat, giving her a once-over. She was young and not Hawaiian. Her nametag read "Jackson," and as she sat, she pulled out a notebook.

"You're Kiki Hepburn, correct?" Officer Jackson asked me.

I nodded.

"Can you tell me anything about last Tuesday night?" she asked.

"I thought Miss Celine had a heart attack?" I said.

Officer Jackson raised her head from her notebook. "Tuesday night?" she prompted, more testily this time.

"Look, I have no problem talking to you about last night, but I deserve to know," I said. "Detective Ray only shows up when there's been a murder. So was Celine murdered?"

Officer Jackson gave me a bored stare. "I'm supposed to ask for details on Tuesday."

"Muuuurddderrrrr," Paulie repeated then clicked his beak in a menacing way.

Officer Jackson stared at the parrot.

The other officer turned around, holding a bottle from the refrigerator. "Jackson, what do you make of this?" He held it up.

I squinted to see what it was. It was a skinny black bottle with two red labels.

Jackson stood and leaned in to look at it. "Bag it," she said before turning back to me. "What happened to the food from that night?"

"It's in the garbage," I said. "Out back. No one felt like eating after Miss Celine got sick." I stood. "Look, I didn't hurt her when I did CPR, did I? Why won't you tell me anything? You expect me to answer questions but won't tell me what's going on?" My eyes stung, and I blinked rapidly to clear them.

"Jackson," Detective Ray said from the doorway. "Go get that trash out back."

Jackson glared at me, stuffed her pretentious little notebook into her back pocket, and stomped out the door.

The other officer held out the bagged bottle to Detective Ray, who glanced at it and nodded. "Note it on the form, please."

Detective Ray turned to me. "Come on in here so we can talk, Kiki."

I put out an arm for Paulie to hop onto then followed Detective Ray into the living room. I wasn't sure where Auntie Akamai went, but I assumed her bedroom or the porch, so after depositing Paulie on the back of Auntie Akamai's favorite chair, I sat on it.

Ray's usual Hawaiian shirt was dominated by orange flowers and had a black background, so I couldn't help but smile that he was wearing Halloween colors. At least until I saw the tiny lime green skulls between the flowers. My smile froze.

Ray followed my stare and flushed. "Yeah, I probably should have changed this shirt."

I shrugged. "Getting in the spirit of a Halloween-themed murder?"

Ray gave a smile that didn't make it to his dark eyes. He seemed to have a few more strands of gray in his hair than last time I saw him, last summer.

"I'll start by saying, no, you didn't do anything to hurt Celine Suzuki," he said. "But while doing routine blood tests during her hospital visit, they found a chemical substance that should not have been in her system. So we need to ask some questions about Tuesday night to see if we can understand how it got there."

I nodded. "I understand. What do you need to know?" I asked.

Detective Ray lifted his notebook. "Just run through the whole night."

"Okay," I said. "The ladies started showing up at six forty-five or so. They do this every week but take turns hosting at their different houses. They seemed to have a routine—they all had a task. I usually leave around the time they start arriving to stay out of the way."

"What is this routine?" Detective Ray asked.

"Well, Celine and Auntie Akamai set up the table and the mahjong tiles and put out the appetizers. Margaux made the drinks, and Oliana made a phone call." I stifled a giggle. "She called in the food order, so maybe that's her contribution to the preparations."

"Why did you stay this time?" Detective Ray made a few more notes and paused to look at me.

"I didn't have anything else to do, and Auntie Akamai asked if I wanted to learn how to play. In case I ever needed to stand in." I stopped, realizing what that sounded like. "Oh, I think if someone travels or gets sick or something…"

Detective Ray gave me a tiny smile. "I know what you meant."

"Oh, okay." I fidgeted and then told myself sternly to sit still. "Okay, so they all showed up, did this little chant and toasted themselves, and then started to play," I said. "Then the food showed up. We passed it out and started eating. They kept playing."

"Did anyone touch another person's food?" Detective Ray asked.

"Well, sure. They took tastes of each other's food. Not mine though. I don't know them well enough to share, you know?" I shrugged.

"Do you know what they had? Each woman?" he asked.

I shook my head. "No, I'm sorry. I'm not really sure. But I'm sure I didn't see any shellfish or shrimp or sea creatures of any kind." I shrugged. "I don't really know what a shellfish allergy entails."

"What did you eat?" Detective Ray asked.

I couldn't help but laugh. "Well, according to this guy here," I said, jerking my thumb over my shoulder at Paulie, "I was eating worms. But it was lo mein."

Detective Ray laughed. "Glad you were not eating worms."

"Me too." I smiled then looked down at my fingernails. "Anyway, at some point, someone—I think Margaux—asked Celine if she was okay. We all looked at her, and she was pale-looking. Then she started to say something and stand but collapsed instead."

Detective Ray nodded and waited for me to go on.

"And then someone said she must have had some shellfish or something, and Margaux got her EpiPen and stuck it in her." I shivered. "She wasn't breathing, so I gave her CPR, and when the ambulance got there, they took over."

Detective Ray nodded. "How did she look at that point?"

"Not good," I said. "She was pale and clammy-looking, but she was breathing again before they took her away."

"And did you notice anything off about the other women?" Detective Ray asked.

I sighed and shook my head. "I don't know them well enough to know if something was weird with any of them."

"Tell me your impressions of them, then," Detective Ray said.

"Well, Celine is—was—very sweet. Super nice, you know?" I glanced up at him, and he nodded. "Margaux is cool, seems a lot younger. Just really funny and cool."

Detective Ray waited a moment then raised an eyebrow. "And Mrs. Harris?"

I grimaced. "Well, she's grumpy. I have to say, I'm surprised she's one of the group. She's so different than the rest of them. Not fun or even pleasant."

"Like what?" Detective Ray asked.

"She was outright mean to the delivery boy, and he turned out to be her grandson! She said his hair was gross or something. Not very grandma-ish, you know?" I lifted my hands in confusion. "And she didn't help clean up or anything, just sat while everyone else did everything. I mean, maybe she's always like that or was really upset about Celine getting sick, but it was kind of strange."

Detective Ray made notes but didn't confirm nor deny that it was strange. "Who made the drinks?" he asked instead.

"Margaux," I said. "She used to be a bartender."

"She mixed the drinks?" he asked, glancing up.

I nodded. "She knew what everyone wanted ahead of time, I guess, and brought those bottles with her. Auntie Akamai usually only has wine here, and that's what she had, I think."

"How about you?" he asked.

"She made me a margarita on the rocks. She said at her house she makes piña coladas when it's her turn to host, but Auntie Akamai doesn't have a blender, so everyone has different drinks, whatever they like."

"What did Celine have?" he asked.

"A mojito. Oliana had a gin and tonic, and Margaux had a dark whiskey mixed thing," I said. "I'm not really sure what it was."

Detective Ray paused in his questions and tapped his pen on his notebook. Finally, he looked up. "Do you know what that bottle in the kitchen was?"

I shook my head. "I've seen it in the refrigerator, and I've seen Auntie Akamai put it in when she's cooking, but I've never read the label." I could feel the heat of a blush creeping up my neck. "I, uh, don't cook. But Auntie Akamai said she'd teach me." I cleared my throat. "What was the bottle?"

Detective Ray blew out a sigh. "It's a common ingredient for Hawaiian cooking, nothing that is unusual to be in the kitchen of every auntie." Now he fidgeted and scratched his neck.

I raised my eyebrows and waited. *And...*

Detective Ray sighed again. "It's oyster sauce."

CHAPTER SIX

After Detective Ray left, I waited for Auntie Akamai to reappear. I didn't have to wait long.

I moved to the couch so she could sit in her usual chair, and she lowered herself into it with a groan.

"What the heck is going on, Auntie Akamai?" I asked her.

"I don't know," Auntie Akamai said tearfully.

Paulie edged his way down to her shoulder and leaned his face against hers. "Sweetums," he crooned at her. "Give us a kiss, sweetums."

Auntie Akamai gave a wan smile and turned her face to her parrot. She puckered up and made a smooch sound, which Paulie immediately echoed.

"Thank you, sweetums," Auntie Akamai said to Paulie and gave the top of his head a little stroke. Then she turned to me.

"I just can't believe someone would have killed Celine on purpose. She was the sweetest woman!" Her eyes filled with tears again, but she blinked them away. "And I certainly can't believe anyone would think I have anything to do with it."

"Oh!" I said. "I don't think Detective Ray thinks you have anything to do with her dying!" I lifted my shoulders in a shrug. "I think he needed to talk to us because it happened here, not because we're suspects. Besides, he never said murder to me. He made it sound like it could have been accidental."

"Did he tell you what they found in her blood?" Auntie Akamai asked me.

I shook my head. "He said something like there was a chemical that shouldn't be there but didn't specify."

She nodded. "I asked. He told me the tests showed digoxin toxicity. I asked if that was just the EpiPen, and he said no." She looked away. "After I went in my room, I searched it on the internet, and it says it could be caused by digitalis."

"What's that?" I automatically reached for my phone but paused. She'd said she already searched it.

"Could be from some flowering plants, but also a drug used for some heart conditions." Auntie Akamai frowned at her lap and crossed her arms. "That's concerning."

"Flowers like…?" I gestured toward the window. "Like some you have?"

She nodded, not making eye contact still. "The foxglove." She glanced up at me. "The one you say looks like Tinker Bell's house?"

"The pink ones?" I asked.

She nodded. "Sometimes they bloom twice a year. And I know they are poisonous to humans." She looked toward the front of the house. "I think Detective Ray may have taken some with him."

I followed her gaze to the front window. "If someone knew they were poisonous and took some from your flowerbed and put them in her food somehow, that's rather spontaneous."

Auntie Akamai nodded. "Honestly, it could have already been in her food. There were purple things that I assumed was purple cabbage."

"You tried her food, didn't you? Did you feel anything?" I asked.

She shook her head. "Not really. I mean, my heart rate went up during the emergency, but I hardly think that was due to something I ate."

I pondered that for a moment. I had to admit, my heart rate certainly went up too. Staying cool under pressure was not the easiest thing, which concerned me should we have an emergency at work. We had a few instances of people getting panicky underwater—clearly a danger—but nothing as bad as this sort of situation.

"How much foxglove would it take to poison someone?" I asked. "And which part of the plant? The blooms or the green parts?"

"I don't know." She shrugged. "And I'm not sure I want to be found with that in my computer search log."

True.

"Would any of your friends already know something like that?" I asked.

Auntie Akamai pursed her lips. "I'm not sure. Margaux does have quite the green thumb. Her garden is beautiful. Usually people who garden a lot know about their plants."

My breath caught in my throat when I realized that Margaux made Celine's drink. It had been a mojito, which comes with muddled mint leaves in the bottom of the glass. Or at least it's supposed to be mint muddled at the bottom of the glass. *Was it foxglove leaves instead?*

My heart in my throat, I looked at Auntie Akamai. She was watching me closely.

"What?" she asked. "Why do you have that face?"

"Margaux made Celine a mojito," I said.

"Yes." Auntie Akamai frowned at me, and then her face cleared when she caught my meaning. "No, no way," she said, shaking her head adamantly. "We've been friends for years. There's no way—or reason—for Margaux to poison Celine. They got along great!"

"What about anyone else? Any hard feelings with anyone?" I asked.

Auntie Akamai shook her head sadly. "There's been disagreements here and there, but nothing worth killing her over."

I raised my eyebrows. "Like what? Who?"

Auntie Akamai looked like she wanted to crawl under the couch. "Celine occasionally showed some backbone to Oliana. Like to tell her to apologize to someone for being rude to them, that sort of thing. Celine was a peacemaker."

"And Oliana a war maker?" I asked then winked to soften the words.

Auntie Akamai sighed. "Let's have some tea. I want more of that pumpkin chai spice you made the other night."

I followed her to the kitchen and sat as she put on the tea kettle. Then she joined me, pulling her light sweater closer around her body. The temperature had certainly changed in the last two months, but it was more of a relief from the heat than anything else. I wouldn't call it cold by any means, but definitely wetter since it rained a lot more. At least, I wasn't cold—that didn't mean Auntie Akamai wasn't.

Auntie Akamai stared at the kitchen tabletop. She absently reached a finger out to rub at a stain. "There are a few ladies at our other mahjong gathering who aren't fans of Celine, but again, they lump her in with Oliana, so it's more Oli than Celine."

I perked up a little. "The mahjong game at the senior center?"

Auntie Akamai nodded. "Yes. Thursdays. There's one woman in particular…" She gazed out the window like she was recalling the scene. "She's always butting into our conversations, staring at us. It's like she has a crush on us." She suddenly shook her head and sighed.

"What?" I asked.

"Celine believed she wanted to join our Tuesday group. Like how Margaux did—or rather, instead of Margaux."

"Margaux joined after the group was established?" I shouldn't have sounded surprised. It's not like I knew the complete history of the group.

"Oh yes." The tea kettle began to whistle, bringing Paulie flapping into the room and imitating the noise. Auntie Akamai hurried over to turn it off so Paulie's sound would also be turned off.

I had introduced Auntie Akamai to the mixture of spices a roommate in Seattle had taught me for a homemade chai, tweaked to add seasonal spices reminiscent of pumpkin pie. I spooned it into mugs, and then Auntie Akamai added the hot water. I carried them to the table after adding spoons to the mugs.

"We three were friends from high school and then college. We had a fourth friend in our little circle, but she moved to the Big Island several years ago." Auntie Akamai stirred her chai while she reminisced. "We met Margaux at the Thursday night mahjong the resort hosts. We hit it off. I mean, who doesn't Margaux hit it off with?" She smiled at me.

I nodded. "She is easy to talk to, that's for sure. Lots of practice in her line of work."

Auntie Akamai nodded. "Yes. So when we decided we would replace our fourth, we all agreed on Margaux." Auntie Akamai frowned at her mug, watching the spices swirl around a moment, and then stirred some more. "The other woman isn't as… pleasant as Margaux."

"Was this other woman upset?" I asked.

Auntie Akamai blew out a breath. "Whoo-eee was she. And I don't blame her, since we went to high school with her too. We were never close or anything though…"

I sensed there was a bit more she hadn't said. "But…?"

"Well, she expected to be invited because she's my next-door neighbor." Auntie Akamai pointed in the direction of the next house. The one occupied by the neighborhood busybody with loose lips.

"Ohhhh," I said, immediately understanding. "Miss Stella." *The gossiping goose.* I didn't blame them at all for preferring the company of Margaux. She was fun, and you wouldn't have to watch what you said in front of her.

"Yes." Auntie Akamai returned her gaze to her tea and stared morosely into it. "I felt awful that she would see us gather here without her then turn around and carpool with her to the senior center."

"Did she *make* you feel bad about that?" I asked.

"Oh yes," Auntie Akamai said. She chuckled. "That woman is an expert-level guilt-tripper."

I tapped my spoon to release its drips then set it on a napkin before taking a careful sip of my hot tea. *Would a guilt tripper become a murderer?*

"Just out of curiosity, why wasn't Stella invited to join? I get not being close friends, but wasn't that the same with Margaux? She is new here, relatively speaking."

Auntie Akamai blew over the top of her cup before taking her first tentative sip. "There's some bad blood between Oliana and Stella."

I raised my eyebrows. "Ooo, spill the tea!"

Auntie Akamai stared at me and then at her teacup.

Chuckling, I shook my head. "It means tell me the gossip."

"Oh." Auntie Akamai nodded. "I don't really know. Neither will say."

"Maybe I should come with you tonight to the senior center mahjong," I suggested. "Watch the other players to see if I get a feel about anyone?"

Auntie Akamai gave me a sly smile. "I think that's an excellent idea. Shall I start a list?"

CHAPTER SEVEN

Auntie Akamai had a pad of paper on the table and was busily writing a list of motives.

She loved this investigation stuff we'd done a few times now, conveniently forgetting the fact that I was the one who got hurt. I even had a couple of scars to prove it.

I sat with my arms crossed, watching her.

She finally glanced up and did a double-take. "What?" she asked, putting down her pen. "I know you said no more investigating, but this one is for me. Not you or Dex this time. This time I might be a suspect." Her eyes pleaded with me.

I blew out a breath. "Of course it's fine. But if I get hurt, you're doing the explaining to my mother."

Auntie Akamai chuckled. "I can handle your mother. Besides, I did the explaining the last two times, didn't I?" She arched an eyebrow.

My parents lived in New York City still, millionaires rolling in old family money (Mother) and hard-earned money (Dad). I grew up with every privilege of that world, except they considered a college degree in anything other than business as an unnecessary endeavor and expected me to either marry rich (Mother) or take over the business (Dad). They wouldn't listen to me about what *I wanted* until I dropped off the grid to scuba dive in various places around the globe. Since that was admittedly on their dime, they sent a private investigator after me, who was, *of course*, murdered. In order to protect myself after being incriminated, I investigated and uncovered the real murderer.

Auntie Akamai gave me a place to live (albeit essentially a shed in her backyard) and helped me when I started looking for the murderer to clear myself.

So, I guess I did owe her.

I pointed at the pad of paper in front of her. "Okay. What have you got so far for motives?"

She glanced down and then sheepishly scratched her neck. "This became a grocery list."

I smirked. "In that case, put cream on it, please."

She noted that then picked up the pad and flipped to a new page. She wrote *motives* in big block letters on the top, made a number one, and then looked at me expectantly.

"Well, heck, I don't know. Did she inspire jealousy? Could it be related to her late husband? Or, like you were saying before, a spot in your mahjong group?" I asked, raising my hands in surrender.

"Cracker!" screamed Paulie in the other room, apparently looking for Auntie Akamai. He strutted into the kitchen. It always made me smile to see him walking.

"Yes, sweetums, I'll get you a cracker," Auntie Akamai said, getting up and going to the counter. She opened the cookie jar of birdseed crackers then paused. "Kiki?" She held up a cracker for me.

"Oh, shush!" I shook my head. It had been literally *six months* since she caught me eating a bird treat. I had thought they were some kind of Hawaiian sesame seed cookies. They were terribly bland, but still. How was I to know?

Auntie Akamai chuckled and sat at the table again after delivering the cracker to Paulie.

"Love," Paulie crooned then made a smooching sound before waddling out of the kitchen again.

"Anyway," Auntie Akamai said, looking back at the notepad. She began to write, but at the number two, she stopped and looked up at me. "What would her late husband have to do with anything?"

"Analise told me Oliana dated him before Celine did," I said. "Seems unlikely there would be any hard feelings after this long, but who knows."

Auntie Akamai stared out into space for several moments before focusing on my face. "Well, heck, I dated him too for a hot second. He wasn't that great for anyone to have held a grudge for a week, let alone thirty years."

"Well, maybe not that one, then," I said.

Auntie Akamai shrugged. "We're brainstorming." She wrote it on the line then moved to number three.

While she was writing, I thought about other reasons people murdered. Anger or revenge? Money?

"Did she have a lot of money?" I asked. "Was someone set to benefit greatly in her will?"

Auntie Akamai tsked. "She was a schoolteacher."

I guess that would be a no, then.

I remembered something I wanted to ask about. "Do you remember Noah's behavior at the gathering?" I asked. "Is that normal for a teenager to sob over his kindergarten teacher?"

Auntie Akamai's eyes went wide. "I thought that was strange, too," she said. "But then I remembered Celine had been very helpful to him after his mother died and, again, when his father remarried. Helped him cope. He would hang out in her classroom as a bigger elementary student. But Celine hadn't mentioned him in years, so I didn't know if she stayed in close contact with him anymore." She shrugged. "I think he outgrew his need for her support."

I nodded. "What about another student or parent from her working years? Anger or revenge for something school-related?" I asked.

Again, Auntie Akamai made a dismissive sound. "She was a kindergarten teacher, so not exactly keeping a kid from college. Unlikely she ever held anyone back or anything or that it would matter if she did, really." She wrote it down anyway then tapped the pen on the paper like a drumstick.

"What other hobbies or clubs was she in? Did she volunteer?" I asked.

Auntie Akamai nodded. "She volunteered with me at the senior center, manning the information desk. And I think at the Nash Animal Shelter." She paused to write those on two lines then wrote a third. When she was done, she looked up. "She was in the gardening club, and yes, there was jealousy there. She had the most gorgeous bougainvillea and was very protective of her plants."

I frowned. *Would someone kill over a plant?* "What do you mean, protective?" I asked.

"Most people might share a plant cutting with their friend, but not Celine. At least not her award-winning bougainvillea," Auntie Akamai said.

"Who wanted it?" I asked. "Do any people come to mind?"

Auntie Akamai froze. She opened her mouth then closed it and cleared her throat. "Margaux," she said in a strangled voice. She cleared her throat again. "But she was never pushy, and they never argued about it." She studied the notepad. "Oh, and her sister."

I stared. "She wouldn't share a plant with her sister?"

Auntie Akamai shook her head adamantly. "No. The clothes off her back, yes. Her lunch, absolutely. A kidney, sure. But her plants? No."

Two things crossed my mind. One, randomly, her sister would get her plants now. Two, this was the second time Margaux and *her* plants had come up.

"I think we need to talk to Margaux," I said. "And what about Stella?"

Auntie Akamai pursed her lips. "I can't fathom Stella wanting to hurt Celine. In high school, she used to follow her around like a puppy. She adored her, and I don't think that changed over the years."

"Was she a jealous friend?" I asked. "We've seen the effects of jealousy of a loved one before."

Auntie Akamai began making little circles in the margin of the paper. "I just don't know if Stella can be devious. Yes, she likes to gossip," Auntie Akamai said, "but she's not malicious."

"We'll see about that," I said. "I might be the next town drunk once she gets around."

CHAPTER EIGHT

Since it was too early for mahjong, we thought we'd run by the animal shelter to talk to Celine's co-workers there. I was at the wheel again, following Auntie Akamai's directions. It was still raining, though now just a steady rain.

I pulled into the parking lot of a small, squat building with a flat roof. Dog runs lined one side, and I could hear the dogs from inside the car.

"What would she do here?" I asked Auntie Akamai.

Auntie Akamai shrugged. "That's something we'll ask. But surely we need to find a way to discuss her without it being suspicious."

"I guess we're looking to adopt a pet, then." I grinned. I had never had a pet, as my mother thought animals were dirty.

We got out of the car, immediately bombarded by the sound of barking dogs.

"Not one of those, I hope," Auntie Akamai called over their noise.

"I meant the role we're playing. I'm not much of a dog person anyway," I said.

"I'm going to be less of a dog person by the time we get out of here!" Auntie Akamai laughed. "I have no idea how Celine volunteered here."

I held open the door for Auntie Akamai and followed her into a vestibule. As directed by a computer-printed sign, we let the outside door close before opening the next one to the inside of the building. I was surprised—and relieved—that it was quieter in here.

"Aloha!" said a chipper middle-aged woman behind the desk. "Welcome to the Nash Animal Shelter. How can I help you today?"

"Aloha," Auntie Akamai responded. "We wanted to see if you had any cats available for adoption." She patted my shoulder. "She misses having a fur baby."

The woman smiled with more teeth than was necessary. "Sure thing. Just head down the hall there, first door on the right. There should be a cat run attendant if you have any questions." She pointed left, away from the dogs.

We thanked her and headed down the hall to the door she had indicated, and which was labeled "cat run" with several cat memes printed out and taped to the door. We opened the door and went inside. The sound of the dogs barking was muffled now but I imagined still enough to make a cat unhappy.

Kennels were stacked three high on both sides of the narrow room. They all appeared empty at first glance, but as soon as the door closed, cats began to pop up from their naps and watched us with big eyes. We walked along the right side first, and cats began hiding or meowing at us, a few going so far as to rub on the cage bars.

"That's pouring it on a little thick, don't you think…Thor?" Auntie Akamai asked one large yellow cat who was rubbing along the bars then flipped over and purred loudly. He reached out a paw to me and slowly blinked his eyes. His cage was labeled with his name and age. They also listed the temperament of the animals, whether or not they liked other pets or children.

Next to Thor was Fluffy, who was anything but. The poor thing was skinny, had a piece of its ear missing, with rheumy-looking eyes.

"Wow," I said, peering at Fluffy and her information sign. "She's twelve! Do you think she's been here all that time?"

"No," said a voice behind us. "She was brought here recently when her owner passed away."

We turned to see a very short older woman smiling up at us.

"Oh, that's sad," I said, turning to glance at Fluffy again.

"Yes," agreed the woman, whose nametag read Linda. "Very sad when the family doesn't keep an animal when the human passes." She raised her hands in surrender. "Not everyone can, I suppose."

Auntie Akamai began talking to her, but I continued down the row, saying hello to each cat. I got to one cage where there were simply green eyes looking out of the darkness of a box in the corner of the kennel. It was a shy one, so I moved on.

I made my way slowly around the whole room, keeping one ear on the conversation between the older women. Auntie Akamai had expertly guided the conversation to Celine.

"Oh, yes, Celine. What a wonderful woman. Such a big heart," Linda said, shaking her head sadly. "Such a shame, taken from us so young."

I turned and looked at her when she said that, a laugh evaporating from my throat when Auntie Akamai narrowed her eyes at me. I quickly returned my attention to the cats, heading back around the room the way I came.

When I got back to the box with green eyes, I leaned in. "You can come out. I'm not gonna hurt you," I said.

The brilliant emerald eyes blinked slowly at me, and then a head and body emerged. An all-gray cat approached me and stretched a paw daintily through the bars. I took the paw and felt its soft fur and even softer foot pads. The cat leaned against the bars so I could pet it.

"Would you like to hold him?" Linda asked.

I glanced at Auntie Akamai, and she gave a quick short nod. "Sure," I said.

Linda opened the kennel and took out the cat. I glanced at its information again. "Loki?" I said. "Is he related to Thor?" I pointed at the yellow cat.

Linda smiled as she turned to me, Loki in her hands. "No, we just have a young man who gives the animals their shelter names. He's quite the superhero movie fan and thought the cat's personality was Loki-like." She looked at Auntie Akamai. "The Norse god Loki, a trickster, not the Hawaiian meaning."

I accepted the cat from Linda and held him awkwardly until he repositioned himself to be more comfortable. He enthusiastically rubbed his face on mine, and I rubbed around his ears and under his chin. He started purring.

"What is Hawaiian Loki?" I asked the women.

"L-O-K-E means flower in Hawaiian," Auntie Akamai explained.

I cuddled him for several minutes before Auntie Akamai announced we needed to go. I tried to hand him back to Linda, but he latched on to my shirt with his claws and didn't want to let go.

Unhooking his claws, paw by paw, Linda was able to get him off me.

My heart constricted as I walked away.

When we stepped into the hall, on full view on the opposite wall was a line of photos for Volunteer of the Month. My hand flew out to stop Auntie Akamai. She turned with raised brows.

I nodded with my chin to one photo and walked over to stand in front of it.

"Well," said Auntie Akamai. "That explains how Noah and Celine were still familiar with each other."

"I agree," I said, studying the photo of a smiling boy holding a small dog that looked like an Ewok from *Star Wars*.

Noah Harris.

* * *

As we drove away from the animal shelter, Auntie Akamai filled me in.

"That volunteer, Linda, had nothing but nice things to say about Celine. No complaints or concerns at all." Auntie Akamai smiled. "As I would expect."

"And now we know how Noah and Celine knew each other still," I added. "They must've worked together a lot."

"Yes, it looks like it," Auntie Akamai said. "All right. Next stop, Margaux's."

We decided offering Margaux a ride to mahjong at the Aloha Lagoon Resort would give us a chance to interrogate—I mean *chat with*—her.

Margaux was waiting on the porch of her modest single-level home when we arrived. Auntie Akamai got out of the car to greet her, and they hugged extra long, and both of them had wet eyes when they got back in the car, Margaux into the back.

The second she got in the car, I knew it wasn't her.

None of her effervescence from the previous times we had met was present.

I looked her over in the rearview mirror. She dug around in her hippie-style sling bag for tissues for her eyes and nose.

"What an awful day I've had," she sniffled.

"What happened?" I asked.

"The police came to my house and interrogated me," she said. "They went through all my cabinets. They said someone poisoned Celine!"

Auntie Akamai made a *tsk*ing sound. "Yes, we know. They told us when they came and looked through our house."

"*And* they took the garbage," I added.

"Well, see, now that makes sense," said Margaux, leaning forward. "To look at what she ate. But to take my bottles? Like I had poisoned my own alcohol? Treating me like a common criminal?" She huffed out a breath.

"I'm sorry, Margaux," I said. "They're just doing their jobs." I couldn't help but wonder if they had also looked at her garden.

"But why would I ever hurt Celine?" she said, dabbing at her face again. "She was one of my best friends and so very nice."

"I agree," said Auntie Akamai in a soothing voice. "But the fact of the matter is, someone did hurt her. Be it accidental or purposeful, someone needs to be held accountable."

Margaux was quiet for a moment then broke the silence with a terrific blow of her nose. "Okay, and did they ask you if you kept poisons for 'religious purposes?'" she asked after wiping her nose.

"*What?*" Auntie Akamai turned around in her seat. "They asked you what?"

"Something to the effect of 'does your religion preclude the use of toxins.' Like what does that even mean?" Margaux said quietly. "But I suppose one cannot be from New Orleans and not be accused of voodoo." She pronounced New Orleans like *N'awlins*.

"Do you practice…that?" I blurted out.

Auntie Akamai turned to me, her mouth open.

"No, no, child," said Margaux. "I was raised in it though. Please know that it is a very misunderstood religion. It isn't full of magic and poison and death. It's not what you see on TV or in the movies at all."

Thankfully, we had arrived at the Aloha Lagoon Resort. We parked in the visitor lot and headed into the resort building.

Once a week, the resort allowed the senior citizens of Aloha Lagoon to gather in one of their ballrooms for their mahjong games. It had started when the senior center was being renovated but continued on as a service to the community.

Just inside the double doors of the ballroom was a check-in table (small cost to cover the cost of the refreshments) that had a large whiteboard with a diagram of the room and the mahjong tables taped to it. Around the room were tables, each with a bag in the center, presumably the mahjong tiles. At the front of the room, by the stage, was a long table with the refreshments. The ladies headed for the white board first, so I followed.

"Do you feel comfortable playing on your own?" Auntie Akamai asked me. She gave me a meaningful look. "So we can *visit with* different people?"

"How many games are played?" I asked.

"Four," Auntie Akamai said. "Here we swap tables between games so we can visit with more people." She pointed at a box on the diagram. "I'll start here. You start there."

Thank goodness I had watched a video online of how to play.

We headed to the drink table, where volunteers were pouring cups of juice. I selected pineapple juice and heard the woman behind me mutter something.

"Excuse me?" I turned around and found myself looking up at a statuesque woman with steel-gray hair, cut short.

"I said you should just hand Oliana Harris a few bucks for the pineapple juice. She owns every pineapple on the island, after all." The woman stared me down. "Who are you?"

"Kiki," I squeaked. "Kiki Hepburn."

"Oh," the woman said, visibly relaxing and losing about two inches of height as she did so. "Akamai's girl."

I wasn't so sure about being Auntie Akamai's "girl," but it was *whatever*.

"You don't like Oliana Harris?" I asked.

"You met anyone who does?" the woman asked, a thin eyebrow arching. "Besides Akamai, I mean. And Celine." She crossed herself then grabbed a drink and hurried away.

I took my juice and went and found the table I was supposed to sit at. No one was there yet, so I chose a chair to wait for my opponents.

Fortuitously for my investigation purposes, Miss Stella, Auntie Akamai's gossipy next-door neighbor and potential suspect, sat down first. She wore a fuchsia cheetah dress (which clashed with both her purple hair tips *and* her neon pink cheetah-print reading glasses) that was almost as loud as her honking voice. She seemed to have forgotten our earlier disagreement for the sake of public appearances, and it was not a surprise that she began to pepper me with questions before her butt even landed in the chair.

"Oh, Kiki," she began. "What a horrible experience for a young girl to go through. It must have been quite terrifying for you!" She lasered her dark eyes on me. "Of course, you've discovered dead bodies twice before, haven't you?" she asked rhetorically—and *loudly*. "You're just a regular dead-body magnet, though both of those bodies were murdered, weren't they?"

I could feel myself shrinking in the chair under the bombardment. I opened and closed my mouth a few times but remained silent.

"Perhaps this last one was murdered too," she whispered at a shout. "Poor, poor Celine. She never did get a break. And her poor, poor family!" she lamented to the entire room.

Several people turned to listen.

"And I heard you were sober enough to give her CPR, yes?" Stella paused long enough to take a breath after firing that volley. "And Margaux gave her the EpiPen." Her eyes narrowed coldly. "I wonder what was in that EpiPen to kill poor Celine."

Okay. *Enough.*

Stella glanced around to make sure people were listening then took a breath to continue.

"What makes you think there was something in the EpiPen?" I interrupted.

"Well, something killed her, right? *Someone?*" Stella raised her eyebrows meaningfully before her eyes shot around to the neighboring tables again.

"You seem to know something that even the police don't know. Who do you suspect?" I asked just as loudly.

Stella leaned forward slightly, and I realized part of the reason she spoke so loudly could be that she was hard of hearing. Probably from hearing herself talk all the time.

"Who do I suspect?" she crowed.

I tipped my head and waited.

A flash of something crossed her face.

"Oh, sweetheart," Stella said loudly, "if I told you who I suspect, I'd be the next victim!" She laughed heartily. *Too heartily.*

Then she glanced around, leaned in close, and whispered a name.

First off, since her breath smelled like booze laced with Listerine, she was really not one to call *me* a drinker. Secondly, the name she hissed at me was *Margaux*.

I leaned back in shock and distaste, but before I could say anything in response, two other women arrived, arm in arm, and sat at our table with us. I wasn't sure what their names were, but they were practiced at handling Stella. One of them immediately shushed her, and then they dominated the conversation by discussing the merits of solar panels for the entire game. Soon enough, the game was over and we took a break to wait for the remaining tables to finish. I headed for the refreshments table again to drown my sorrows in more pineapple juice.

There was a large clump of seniors gathered around one, and it didn't take but a second to see that Oliana Harris was holding court. For all the hate the woman garnered behind her back, people were overly solicitous to her face. I heard concerned murmurs from the throng as they listened to her recount Celine's last moments—or at least her last moments at the mahjong game at Auntie Akamai's house.

I stood at the edge of the cluster of women. I recognized a woman close to Oliana as the very tall woman who hated pineapples, but she was singing a different tune now, as my grandmother would say. I got a sudden flash of recognition. This was exactly like high school.

That revelation caused me to physically take a step back.

"Whoa there, Kiki." Auntie Akamai put her hand on my back to stop me from mashing her toes.

I turned to her. "This reminds me so much of high school," I whispered, glancing back over my shoulder. "I thought people matured past this stuff."

Auntie Akamai laughed. "No, my girl, some never do."

A hand bell was rung by a woman near the stage. "Five minutes," she said.

Women began to trickle back to tables, so I turned to scope out where I should go next.

"Kiki, dear, come sit with me," a voice said, and a gnarly hand with a steel grip clamped on to my arm. "Let's go over here."

I had little choice then to let Oliana Harris drag me away.

CHAPTER NINE

"Mrs. Harris, how are you doing tonight?" I asked Oliana as we wound our way through tables. Several people tried to stop her to talk, but she ignored them. And me.

"Goodness, these people are vultures," she hissed. "Vultures!"

I sat where I was told and waited for her to continue.

"All they want to know are details about Celine," Oliana said. "Like vultures watching a traffic accident, waiting to eat up the gore!"

Disgusting image, but I got her drift.

"There wasn't any gore," I said.

"Yes, darling, I know, but they want to know dirt." She glanced around then leaned toward me. "One woman even asked me if I thought one of us was responsible. As if that were possible!" Her eyes flashed with indignation.

"Really?" I said. "Even Auntie Akamai?"

"Oh, yes. Even *you*," she said.

"*Me?*" I gasped.

Two women started to sit then saw who was sitting there already and pretended to see someone calling them. "Coming!" one said loudly to no one in particular, and they both hurried away.

Yup. Just like high school.

"Yes, especially you. One woman is saying you're a dead body magnet," Oliana said, shaking her head.

"Oh. Right." I nodded. "Stella. She said it straight to my face."

Oliana frowned at me, and I thought I saw a hint of something like compassion grace her face for a moment. "That woman is a menace," she said in lieu of something nicer, like *you're not a dead body magnet*.

"What do you think happened?" I asked.

She looked at me, surprised. "I think something gave her an allergic-like reaction, which we interpreted as an actual allergic reaction. Then that substance interacted with her EpiPen, causing her heart attack," Oliana said, like she was stating a fact instead of an opinion. "I have a call in to the coroner to discuss my theory."

I didn't hide my reaction as well as I thought. I was thinking *how imperious and entitled is this woman?*

After a glance at my face, a smile flitted across her lips. "I was a bio-chem major in college and flirted with the idea of medical school. And the coroner and I have tea once a week."

"Oh, I didn't know that," I said truthfully. "Why didn't you go to medical school?"

Oliana sighed and looked down at her tiles, choosing to ignore my question. "We may as well set up for two players. I think people are avoiding the dead body magnet and the wicked witch of Aloha Lagoon."

* * *

I didn't learn much that night, other than why Auntie Akamai liked Oliana Harris. One-on-one with her, we got along fine. She was astute and had a sarcastic wit that yes, left scorch marks if you didn't read the sarcasm in it.

I *liked* her. And it surprised me.

Something else that surprised me was after the third game, I looked up to see Detective Ray watching from the stage. He wasn't hiding behind the curtain or anything, but he certainly wasn't standing out in plain view.

I decided to skip the fourth game and see what I could learn from him instead. I got an extra cup of juice and made my way up the small staircase on the side of the stage, joining him near his watching post.

He smiled and accepted the offered cup of juice. Tonight, his Hallo-waiian–print shirt had a purple background with grinning jack o' lanterns scattered amongst fuchsia hibiscuses and teal surfboards.

"Glad to see you don't think I'm a poisoner," I said, nodding my chin at the cup in his hand.

"I watched you pour it. Unless you're really slick, I didn't see you add anything to it," he said.

My mouth dropped open, and he laughed.

"I'm kidding," he said. "I don't think you're a poisoner."

I rolled my eyes and turned to look out over the group of senior citizens. I had noticed a few men, but there were mostly women in the room.

"So, do you usually hang with the over-sixty crowd at mahjong?" he asked me.

I shook my head. "No, we just thought it might be fun," I said.

"Or you thought you might learn something about Celine's murder," Detective Ray said.

I peeked at him, but he was still facing forward. *Was he kidding or serious?*

"No, of course not," I lied.

"Did you learn anything interesting in the course of the *fun*?" he asked, lifting his pinky finger from his juice cup to make a halfhearted air quote around "fun."

"Mostly that little old ladies and high school girls aren't that different," I said. "You've got your mean girls, your gossips, your beauty queens…"

Detective Ray laughed.

"And everyone loved Celine, and no one seems to have wanted her dead," I said.

Detective Ray nodded. "Yes, that's going to make it a challenge to find the killer, isn't it?"

My eye was caught by the tall, imposing woman with the steel-gray hair. "Most of them seem to dislike Oliana Harris though. And aren't afraid to say it—behind her back, at least."

"Just like high school," Detective Ray murmured.

The last games were coming to an end and Detective Ray slipped behind the curtain, so I left and went in search of Auntie Akamai.

On the way home in the car, Auntie Akamai didn't ask about any investigation-type things until we had dropped off Margaux. The festivities of the night hadn't cheered Margaux up at all. It was odd to see her down, and Auntie Akamai agreed.

"People are talking about her, and she feels like an outsider right now," Auntie Akamai explained after we dropped off Margaux.

"Did you learn anything interesting?" I asked.

"Just one thing," she said. "Do you remember the coroner? You met her last summer?"

By last summer, she meant the time Detective Ray asked me to confirm the identity of a murder victim.

"Dr. Yoshida?" I asked. "Yes, I remember her."

Auntie Akamai glanced around as if checking for eavesdroppers, even though we were alone in the car. "Well, Dr. Yoshida's mother's cousin's neighbor was here tonight and said something rather alarming to the player opposite the woman next to me in the third game."

I need a diagram for that.

"Dr. Yoshida's mother… Okay, what was the alarming thing?" I asked.

"That the chemical in Celine's blood was, or maybe was similar to, digitalis." Auntie Akamai crossed her arms and looked at me expectantly.

"The Tinker Bell plant?" I asked.

"Well, yes. The scientific name for foxglove is digitalis. But apparently, it is also the name of a heart medication. Maybe the medication has the plant or its extracts in it. I don't know." Auntie Akamai flapped a hand to dismiss the thought. "The point is, Celine didn't take a heart medication."

"So she ingested it somehow, and when we thought she was having an allergic reaction, she was really having a reaction to the digitalis?" I asked. *Just like Oliana said.*

"Exactly." Auntie Akamai nodded. "The part I'm unclear on is why they told us she had a heart attack. Did they not want to tell us she was poisoned?"

"They probably didn't know right away," I pointed out. "And how could she have a heart attack if given medicine that I am assuming keeps you from having a heart attack?"

Auntie Akamai shook her head. "We need to do some research, I guess."

"Did you by any chance talk to Oliana tonight?" I asked.

"Sure, a little. Not much about this." She looked at me. "Why?"

"Because she has a theory that she says she thought up that sounds very much like what the phone tree of people relayed from Dr. Yoshida." I slowed to a halt at a four-way stop and, uncertain when it was my turn, overstayed my welcome.

"Go, Kiki," Auntie Akamai said testily. "And finish explaining."

"Oliana said she thought the substance made us think she was having an allergic reaction, but she wasn't, then the EpiPen interacted with the substance to kill her," I said after we were on our way again.

"Did Oliana say digitalis?" Auntie Akamai asked.

"No, I don't think so," I said. "Why?"

"Remember that night, when they told us Celine had a heart attack and Oliana said it should have been her, not Celine?"

"Yes, I think so," I said. "I think she said she had a bad heart, right?"

"Right," confirmed Auntie Akamai. "Want to take a guess what medicine Oliana takes for her heart?"

"Oh no," I said. I was just starting to like the old grouch.

"Oh, yes," said Auntie Akamai. "Oliana takes digitalis."

CHAPTER TEN

The next morning, I woke to the smell of frying Spam. That meant the day's dive excursion was on.

The thought of diving usually propelled me out of bed like a cartoon character, but I actually felt a little disappointed. Auntie Akamai and I were supposed to do some research. When we got home the night before, Auntie Akamai was worn out, physically and emotionally. She didn't have the drive to research like she had in the past, so we agreed to do it today, forgetting I might, in fact, have to work.

I dragged myself out of bed and to the bathroom. I braided my thick hair in two pigtails and threw some sweatpants and a sweatshirt over my usual swimsuit. It wasn't cold enough to need a wetsuit to dive, but these early mornings could get a little chilly.

I got to the kitchen as she was wrapping up the sandwiches.

"Good morning, Auntie," I said. "How did you sleep?"

"All right. And you?" Auntie Akamai was focused on the food, but once she was done wrapping, she looked up at me.

"Fine," I said. I fetched the foldable crate from the pantry, and we loaded it with the sandwiches, chips, and oranges. The dive shop kept a supply of bottled water there for those who didn't bring their own reusable ones like we recommended.

As we were finishing, Dex arrived. He verbally sparred with Paulie on his way through the living room, as usual, then gave us both kisses on the cheek.

"You are feeling better now, *keiki*?" Auntie Akamai asked after patting his cheek.

Dex grinned. "Yes! Just in time for the weekend, right?" He winked at me. "Not that we get one, really."

We usually ran a dive two to three days during the work week and then both Saturday and Sunday afternoons.

Dex hefted up the crate, and Auntie Akamai and I followed him to the door.

"We'll talk more about…stuff…when I get home, okay?" I said to her.

She nodded. "I'll wait for you."

After Dex and I were in his Jeep and on the road, he turned to me. "So what was that all about? What do you need to talk about?"

"Oh, you know." I shrugged. "Looks like it should be a nice day today, huh?" I turned and looked out the side window.

"Oh, no, no, don't you try to redirect me," Dex chuckled. "What little plans are you guys hatching, and does it have anything to do with Miss Celine dying?"

I turned to look at him. "She was murdered, Dex."

"*What?*" Dex swerved slightly when he snapped his head to look at me. "What are you talking about?"

"Someone poisoned her," I said. "Or at least she had some toxic substance introduced to her system. I think that's how Detective Ray worded it."

"Oh, wow." Dex shook his head. "That's crazy. Who would want to murder Miss Celine? She's the best." He froze for a moment. "*Was* the best."

"I don't know what to tell you, Dex," I said. "Someone gave her something."

"That's really surprising," he said.. "I mean, if any of them were to be murdered, I'd expect it to be Oliana Harris."

"Oh, stop!" I slapped his arm playfully. "Don't say anything so awful! I actually kind of like Oliana."

"Really?" Dex said, laughing. "Have you met her?"

"Oh, she's not that bad," I said. "Did you know she wanted to go to medical school? Said she was accepted but didn't go. When I asked why, she changed the subject."

"Interesting, considering she certainly never needed to have a job, being the Pineapple Princess and all." Dex steered the Jeep into its usual spot behind the dive shop and put it in Park.

I crossed my arms and gave him a look. Had I ever told him the New York paparazzi had called me the "Property Princess" for a few years?

Dex turned off the ignition and pulled the key out then noticed I was glaring at him. He stared back into my eyes for a few long moments.

"Sorry," he said. "Point taken. Okay then, on that note. Let's go to work."

Together we went to the dive shop entrance, where we were met by our boss and Dex's dad, Kahiau. Since there were already clients arriving, I went straight behind the counter to do the diver registration.

Twenty minutes later, I went out to talk to Kahiau. "We're ready," I told him. "Everyone arrived early."

Kahiau's eyebrows shot up. "Wow, good. Let's go, then."

Everyone piled into the van, and Dex drove to the marina.

"How's my sister doing?" Kahiau asked me in a quiet voice.

"Auntie Akamai's okay," I whispered back. "Obviously upset, of course, and it doesn't help they are investigating the death, to include going through her cabinets."

"Dex updated me," Kahiau said. "But what were they looking for?"

I shrugged. "I don't know, but they took some oyster sauce from the refrigerator."

"Oyster sauce," said Kahiau, leaning back upright. "Yeah, I get that. So they must think someone purposefully gave her something she was allergic to?"

"Something like that," I said. I saw no need to mention the digitalis, since I didn't know for a fact that it was involved.

"I can't think why someone would do that," he said. "Everyone loves Celine."

"Well, one person at least didn't," I said dryly.

Kahiau studied me. "I suppose not. Unless there was some kind of mistake."

"Mistake?" I stared at him. "What do you mean, a mistake?"

He shrugged. "If everyone loved Celine and no one would want to hurt her, maybe she wasn't supposed to be hurt?"

"Hmm." I looked out the window to ponder, and a client leaned forward to talk to Kahiau.

It was an interesting idea, but my memories of the night played over in my head. Celine distributed our meals to us, so it was unlikely she took the wrong one. The appetizers were made by Auntie Akamai and me, so I knew their ingredients. The "mummy dogs" were pigs in a blanket made with prepackaged cocktail weenies and the dough from those pastry tubes that terrified me. (It had been my first experience opening one of those tubes, and when the tube popped open, it scared me out of my flip flops!) The "bloody fingers" were shortbread cookies with a sliced almond for a fingernail, served with a variety of dips, including a blood-like sticky red jam. We made the cookies, but though something could have been added to one of the dips, we all took some.

There was only one thing made specifically for Celine, and I didn't witness its creation.

Her cocktail.

* * *

It was a beautiful day and a perfect dive. Our excursion was over much too quickly.

As we pulled alongside the dock, my phone dinged with a text from Auntie Akamai.

Meet me at the shelter after work, it said.

I shot a quick *ok* back to her and let Dex know.

"Why?" asked Dex. "Not that I have a problem with it. I've been thinking about getting a dog anyway."

"Really?" I grabbed the folded lunch crate from under the bench where I had tucked it. "I never knew that."

He shrugged. "Mom never wanted one around, but now that I'll be getting my own place…" He grinned. He waggled his eyebrows at me.

Dex had been searching for an affordable apartment for quite some time but hadn't been able to find one. Recently though, he got a tip about one coming available at the end of December. Whether or not he got it remained to be seen.

After finishing everything on our post-dive checklist, we climbed into the Jeep and headed for the animal shelter. Auntie Akamai had never said why exactly she needed me there, but as we pulled up, it became obvious. There were a dozen cars in the lot this time, compared to the two or three last time, and there were people walking around in an aimless manner.

"What is going on?" Dex asked as he drove into a parking spot under a tree.

Just then, a dog went flying by the Jeep, chased by a woman holding a bag of dog treats.

"I guess animals got loose?" I watched in the side mirror as the dog circled around and headed back to the building, still pursued by the woman. Moving quickly, I hopped out of the Jeep, leaving the door open, and knelt in the path of the dog.

Surprisingly, the dog stopped, tail wagging and tongue lolling out of its mouth. I reached up to pet it, rubbed its ears, and then took hold of its collar.

The woman came up, panting as much as the dog was. "Thank you," she gasped. I recognized her purple tips immediately and realized it was Stella, Auntie Akamai's next-door neighbor.

"No problem," I said. "What happened here?"

"A volunteer decided to let out all the animals," Stella said and shook her head in disgust. "Silly boy."

"Boy?" I asked. "Do you mean Noah Harris did this?"

She nodded, grasped the dog's collar, and began to coax it toward the building. "No clue what got into him."

Dex came around the side of the Jeep to join me and pointed to the far edge of the building. "There's my aunt."

Auntie Akamai was bent over and only recognizable by the colorful print of her dress. We walked toward her. Once we got close enough, we could see she was trying to tempt a cat with a can of tuna.

I put out a hand to stop Dex so we wouldn't scare the cat off. "We're here, Auntie," I called softly.

"Oh, good," she said, groaning as she straightened up. "My back can't take this." She took the few steps toward us and handed me the open can. "You can try."

I approached the bush she had been bending near and squatted. Peering under the branches, I could see a cat—the skinny, raggedy one with the unlikely moniker.

"Fluffy," I called to it in a sing-song voice. "Come get some nummy tuna."

The cat regarded me with his foggy eyes then limped forward to sniff the can. I let him take a lick and eat a little piece before I eased forward and picked him up. Cradling Fluffy in my arms, I turned around.

"Now what?" I asked.

Auntie Akamai rolled her eyes. "That stubborn thing came right to you." She pointed at the front door. "Just take it in to its kennel."

Auntie Akamai and Dex went off after a dachshund going warp speed on its tiny legs, and I went into the building. Turning left, I went to the cat room and put Fluffy back in his home. I gave him a little pile of tuna from the can and then closed and latched the door. I made a quick tour of the room and saw there were still several missing cats, including Thor and Loki, the two over-lovable ones. I headed back outside.

As I was passing the front desk, a display on the wall caught my eye. A small plaque commemorated a substantial donation by Oliana Harris to the shelter, in memory of her husband, Nathan. In fact, the shelter was named the Nathan A.S. Harris Animal Shelter—the NASH Animal Shelter. I facepalmed. Why hadn't I noticed that before? It wasn't *Nash*. It was *NASH*, Oliana's late husband's initials.

"What's wrong?" a voice said.

I turned toward it and found myself face-to-face with Margaux LaRoux. "Oh, nothing. I just didn't realize this facility was named for Oliana's husband," I said.

She nodded. "Yes, apparently he went by the nickname Nash." She picked a handful of dog treats out of a box sitting open on the counter. "Which was his initials." She shrugged. "I've heard of worse nicknames."

Together we walked out the door.

"You must be a cat-catcher," Margaux said, nodding to the can in my hand. "There's still so many loose. The dogs terrorized them. Several are in trees."

"How about dogs? How many of them are still loose?" I asked her.

"Seven, if I counted the empty runs correctly," Margaux said. "A couple are kind of scary dogs too. The animal control guys will probably have to get them. Won't do to have even more wild dogs out there."

Apparently, the non-scary dachshund Dex went after got tired of being chased by Dex's long legs and gave up. Dex walked toward us holding him.

Margaux held out her arms. "I know which kennel he goes in," she said and took the little dog from his arms. The dog stared longingly over Margaux's shoulder at Dex as she carried him away.

"I feel you, dog," I said with a smile and threw my arms around Dex's neck and gave him a big smooch.

"Okay," said Dex, smiling down at me. "What was that for?"

I shrugged out of his arms. "Just 'cause." I pointed at a tree. "Margaux said the dogs treed a lot of cats, so let's look up."

We wandered around, peering up into trees and bushes for another half hour, but didn't see any more animals hiding.

Finally, Auntie Akamai approached us. "Thank you for coming to help," she said. "This is such a shame. I don't know what

Noah was thinking!" She shook her head angrily. "If he really cared about the animals, he would have thought about their well-being, and this is certainly not good for that!"

"Why did he do it?" I asked.

"No idea," she said. "He apparently came in early and did it and then reported it to the police. Even confessed to doing it."

"Did he break a law?" Dex asked.

Auntie Akamai shrugged. "I've no idea. The shelter certainly won't charge him with anything, you know…Oliana and all." She shook a fist. "I have half a mind to put that boy over my knee, I am telling you right now."

That mental image almost made me smile, but I decided that wouldn't be a good move.

Auntie Akamai swung her head around to look at me as though she had read my mind. She pursed her lips and glared but didn't say anything.

I opened my eyes wider to feign innocence. "It sounds like he was looking for attention, acting out for some reason."

Auntie Akamai relaxed a little. "Yes, I'd have to agree. But why?"

"Well, none of us are child psychologists, and he's not our kid, so not really our problem, right?" Dex said.

"Well…" I tipped my head, thinking. "Unless it has something to do with the murder."

Auntie Akamai nodded. "That had crossed my mind when I was on my hands and knees looking in the storm drain," she said. "He could be trying to distract attention away from it, though this isn't nearly worth dropping a murder investigation."

"Or he's just super mad at his grandmother," said Dex.

"I think he could be mad at her, but I don't see how it would connect to the murder," I said. "He has reason to be upset with her. She isn't very nice to him."

"They're fine," scoffed Auntie Akamai. "She just doesn't like his hair. Or clothes. Or friends…" She paused. "Well, on second thought, you are right. She isn't very nice to him, is she?"

The woman from the desk the first day came out of the building. "I think this is all we're going to get for now. I'll set up volunteers to stay the night in case any come back at night for dinner or to sleep."

Auntie Akamai went to talk to her, while Dex and I headed for the Jeep. I was embarrassed to see I had left the passenger-side door open. Dex had recently put the top on the Jeep since it was the rainy season, but the sides were still open, so he probably wouldn't care about the door being open.

We agreed on dinner at Sir Spamalot's, our go-to date place. I was not the best company though, as I was preoccupied and it showed.

"Earth to Kiki," Dex said in his deep, sexy voice.

"Sorry." I smiled at him. "Just thinking about something your dad said earlier."

"What?" he asked. "You have a faraway look in your eyes because you're thinking about my *dad*?" He feigned being affronted.

"Don't be silly," I said, rolling my eyes. "I said something he *said*, not his manly good looks or inviting smile."

The smile disappeared from Dex's face, and I couldn't help but laugh.

"I'm joking around." I reached across the table and took his hand. "I only think about *your* manly good looks and inviting smile. Don't worry."

Dex looked relieved, which made me want to roll my eyes again. "So, what did he say?" he asked.

"He said something to the effect of maybe Celine wasn't the intended victim. That everyone seemed to love her, so maybe her dying was a mistake." I shrugged. "But I am starting to have concerns about Celine being poisoned by someone close, and it definitely would not have been a mistake."

Dex frowned. "Go on."

I sighed. "The only thing Celine ate or drank that wasn't made by Auntie Akamai or the restaurant—which Celine handed out the food from—was her cocktail." At the word cocktail, I leaned forward and took a sip from my soda.

Realization dawned in Dex's eyes. "And her cocktail was made by..."

I nodded. "Margaux."

Dex looked away from the table as he considered. "What did she drink?"

"That's what has me concerned," I said. "Margaux made her a mojito. You know how it has the mashed mint leaves at the bottom?"

"Can't say I've ever had one," he admitted. "But I have seen them. So you're concerned it wasn't mint? What would it be?"

"Foxglove," I said. "It could be in Margaux or Celine's flower garden. I haven't gone looking yet. It certainly is in Auntie Akamai's."

"Foxglove?" Dex repeated. "It could have killed her?"

I shrugged. "The substance in her system, according to Detective Ray, was a digoxin toxin. The real name for the plant is digitalis. I think we can assume that's the same substance since a lot of medicines come from plants."

"Wait," Dex said. "They could be growing poisonous plants in their garden? Why?"

"They're pretty?" I said. "They could have oleander, and I remember from reading a book or a movie or something that it's poisonous too. A lot of pretty things are deadly."

"Well," he said, reaching across to take my hand again, "I'm glad my pretty thing isn't deadly."

I smiled. "Flattery will get you nowhere."

Dex's dark eyebrows rose. "Are you sure about that?" he teased.

I gave him a flirtatious look and flipped my hair. "We'll see."

"I have an idea…" Dex leaned forward and lowered his voice. "I know of a romantic spot we could sneak off to."

CHAPTER ELEVEN

Dex's idea of "romantic" was...*interesting*. Unless, of course, he meant romantic like swashbuckling pirates and adventure.

"Whose place is this?" I asked, staring at the dark lot with a small house. It was surrounded by a bountiful garden, so I had a feeling I already knew the answer.

"Margaux's," Dex said. "I know she's not home, so I thought we could poke around the yard a little."

"How do you know she's not here?" I asked.

"She picks up a shift at The Lava Pot on occasion, and she mentioned she'd be there tonight when we spoke at the shelter." He looked over at me. "Are you scared?" He said it in a taunting tone I did not appreciate.

"No, I'm not scared. I just don't want to be weird and nosy," I said. "She trusts us. And what if someone sees us?"

Dex shrugged. "We say we're dropping something off. I don't know."

I stared at him a good long moment then sighed. "Okay. Let's be quick."

Dex reached across and opened his glove box, causing an avalanche of rubber duckies to pour out and onto the floor. It was a "Jeep thing," or so I'd read, that Jeep drivers put miniature rubber ducks on other people's Jeeps.

"Dex!" I laughed. "You do know you're supposed to put those on other Jeeps, right?"

"I know. I just like them. They're cute," he laughed. "Can you grab the flashlight?"

I dug around for the flashlight and handed it to him then gathered up the dozen or so duckies that were on the floor to stuff back in the glove box.

We got out of the Jeep and closed the doors quietly then crept up the short sidewalk. Dex opened the gate for me then left it in the closed but unlatched position.

"Do you know what these plants look like?" Dex asked me.

I nodded. "Like bells… I think they look like Tinker Bell's house," I explained. "Pink, maybe light-purple flowers."

I heard Dex chuckle in the darkness. "Tinker Bell, eh?"

We moved through the dark garden, following paths lit by small solar lights that didn't do much to help but did create a little light for us to see the nearest plants.

I stopped next to some waist-high bell-shaped blooms. "I think this is the plant," I whispered.

Dex knelt next to it and turned on his cell phone flashlight. He began inspecting the plant from top to bottom. "Is it the blooms or the leaves that are poisonous?" he asked.

"Oh." I froze. "I have no idea."

"Well," Dex said quietly, "if it's the leaves, we might have a problem." He pointed to the side of the plant, where it appeared several leaves had been removed.

"Take a picture," I said.

After he took a few shots, we straightened and continued on. I stopped again next to a shrub and took a quick picture of its leaves, and did so with the next two as well.

Dex interrupted my flora photo shoot. "Look, Kiki, there's a little house."

I glanced up. "Maybe a gardening shed?"

Dex was already walking toward it. "More like a greenhouse."

I caught up to him as he was peering through the window. I cuddled up to his arm and tried to look through as well. "What's in there?" I asked, holding a hand above my eyes to look in.

"Looks like some jars and pots, but I don't know what's in them," Dex said. "The door has a padlock, so we can't go in, unfortunately."

"That is unfortunate. I wish I could see that plant there more clearly," I said, pointing at a branch in a jar. It had blooms, but I couldn't see much detail in the dark.

"Does this help?" Dex asked, holding up his phone and pressing on the flashlight. He laid it against the window.

"Yes," I gasped. "It does, and what gorgeous flowers."

"I think that's bougainvillea," Dex said. "My mom loves the stuff."

"Bougainvillea?" I repeated dumbly. I stared at the blooms. *Was there any way to find out if these were from Celine's plants?*

"Let's go," I whispered. "I don't want to press our luck."

We crept back toward the front of the house, and after stepping through the gate, Dex quietly latched it.

"Excuse me!" said a shrill voice. "What are you doing in there!?"

I jumped as I spun around. It was the tall woman with the steel-gray hair from mahjong at the senior center. I hoped desperately that Dex had thought of an excuse by now.

"Good evening, ma'am. We were looking for an escaped cat," said Dex. "Did you hear about all the escaped animals from the shelter today?"

The woman, eye level with Dex, narrowed her eyes at him. "Uh-huh. You mean the cat sitting on that Jeep?" She pointed at Dex's Jeep, which he had parked right in front of Margaux's house. *Real sneaky.*

Dex and I turned, and sure enough, a dark-colored cat was sitting on the hood.

"Oh, yes!" I cried and hurried toward the Jeep, slowing as I approached. "Loki, there you are!"

The cat gave a plaintive *meow* as it regarded me with its green eyes.

"Thank goodness!" I reached for the cat, and he didn't dart away, so I took him into my arms. "You little stinker!" I turned back to the tall woman. "He's called Loki for a reason! Very mischievous."

The woman looked at me with suspicion. "We're miles from the shelter. How'd he get over here?" She reached forward and rubbed his head between his ears. "Sweet guy though."

"He jumped out the window," Dex said, coming over to us and staring at the cat.

The woman looked at Dex like she wouldn't trust him any farther than she could throw him. Which, since she looked like an East German shot-putter, could have been a decent distance. "Mmhm," she grunted. "Well, you found him, so you best be off now."

We agreed, murmured good nights, and got back into the Jeep. Loki sat on my lap like he belonged there, staring up at me, then butted my chin with his head.

"Thank you, Loki," I said, stroking his soft fur. "You got us out of that jam. But what do we do with you now?"

Dex pulled away from the curb and gave a jaunty wave to the tall woman, who stood with her arms crossed. "I hope the old bat doesn't say anything to Margaux," he muttered.

"Oh, Dex," I said, still loving on Loki. "Don't call her an old bat. I'll be old someday too, you know, as will you."

"For one, I look forward to seeing you old," Dex said, glancing at me. He hurriedly added, "Plus, she's always been an old bat. She was our principal at the high school."

"Oh gosh," I said, skimming over the first part of his statement. "Does she know who you are?"

"I think so. That's why she looked so distrustful of me," Dex laughed as he turned the corner at the end of the street. "I was a good kid, but Tiny and I got into some fun, you know?"

Tiny, his not-so-tiny childhood friend who was now starting his first year in professional football, could probably hold his own with the tall woman.

"She's definitely an imposing figure. I can see her as a principal, no problem," I said.

Dex rolled to a stop at a stop sign. "So what are we doing with the cat?" he asked.

"Well, the shelter lady did say someone would be there to let in the ones that came back for food or shelter," I said. "She should still be there."

Dex nodded and turned on his blinker to go left.

And Loki sprang from my arms and out the open window frame.

"Sonofa…" I leaned out the window to watch him run down the sidewalk in the opposite direction. "Dex! What do we do?"

Dex blew out a breath then put the blinker to go right instead, rounded the corner, and pulled to a stop at the curb. "Let's go see if we can get him back, I suppose."

We got out of the Jeep and backtracked down the road. Loki was simply sitting on the sidewalk until we got close enough, then would turn and sprint farther down the street, and then repeat his sitting.

On his third sprint, he stopped to greet a woman walking toward us.

"Kiki?" the woman said. "Is this your cat?" She picked him up.

I squinted at her. "Analise?"

"Hey Analise," said Dex. "How are you?"

She nodded her greeting to Dex. "So-so. Just checking on my aunt Celine's house." She gestured with a hand while her arms held Loki against her body. He rubbed his face in her long hair.

"This is Loki," I said, pointing at the cat. "He's quite the troublemaker. He got out of the shelter today and then just showed up on the hood of the Jeep. We were going to take him back to the shelter, but he jumped out the window."

The cat turned his head and gave me a look.

Analise tutted. "I think he wants to be with you, Kiki." She smiled and rubbed his ears. "Not the shelter."

I looked at the house we were standing in front of. It was Celine's. *Hmmm.*

"Analise, you know about your aunt's bougainvillea plants?" I asked her.

"The award-winner? Sure." She tipped her head. "Want to see it?"

"Actually, yes," I said. "If you don't think that's a problem."

"Not at all," said Analise. "It's really pretty. I love it. It smells nice too."

Still holding Loki, she led us up the front walk and around to the back. Celine also had a shed, but Analise walked right past it to a small fenced area. "There…" Analise pointed.

I opened the knee-high gate and went in to see the bush up close. Analise followed me.

"Oh, no!" she cried. "This is crazy. I'm going to kill my mom!"

"What?" I asked. But based on the condition of the bush, I figured I knew the answer.

Several branches had been removed, almost looking like it had been pruned, and blossoms littered the grass under it.

CHAPTER TWELVE

Analise raged on about her mother taking cuttings of the beautiful shrub before her aunt was even buried.

"Maybe she took some to put on Celine's grave? Or took them for the funeral?" suggested Dex, but he went unheard by Analise.

"It wasn't necessarily your mom," I said, thinking back to the branch in the jar at Margaux's. "Anyone could have come into the yard and taken some."

Analise calmed. "That's true. What scavengers though, you know? Ugh." She pushed Loki into my arms. "That really upsets me."

Obviously! I cradled Loki, holding him tightly this time as we went back out of the fence and waited for Analise to close the small gate, now that my arms were full.

"They do smell amazing," I said. "And they're really pretty."

"She developed her own variety," Analise said and sniffled. "She named it after me." She wiped at her eyes. "*Bougainvillea Analise*. It won an award last year."

I reached a hand to her shoulder to comfort her, but taking advantage of my loosening my grip, Loki jumped out my arms and darted away.

"Not again," Dex muttered. "Stupid cat."

"He clearly does not want to go back to the shelter," I said. "I'm not sure what we can do about it now."

Together, the three of us walked to the sidewalk.

"Have you heard about the Halloween wedding?" Analise asked me.

I nodded. "The bridal party was diving with us a few days ago. She invited us."

"Yeah, I got an invite too," Analise said. "I met them in the bar, and they invited me and my friend. They said to invite others as we saw fit."

"Why?" asked Dex. "Do they want a ridiculously large crowd?"

Analise shook her head. "She said not many of her friends were able to come because the wedding was in Hawaii, and a lot of the family wasn't supportive of the distance or the theme. They are practically eloping."

"That's pretty crazy," I said. I looked around to see if Analise had a car.

Dex did the same. "Do you need a lift home?" Dex asked.

Analise shook her head. "It's not far. I could use the walk to cool down before I get home and see my mom." She gave a little wave as she turned. "Night!"

We walked in the opposite direction, back toward the Jeep.

After getting in, Dex just sat and looked at me.

"So are you thinking what I think you're thinking?" he asked.

"Probably," I admitted. "That Margaux took a branch from the bougainvillea to start one of her own."

"Does it work that way?" he asked.

"For some plants, I think," I said. I had taken some botany classes in college, but this still required the expertise of the all-knowing internet. I pulled out my phone and did a quick search. "Yes, you can grow one from a cutting. Looks like that's also the method to develop new varieties." I grinned at him. "And I was really not getting the spelling of bougainvillea anywhere near correctly in my mind."

"Boo-ganvilla?" Dex laughed. "Getting in the mood for the season?"

I giggled with him. "Boo!"

"You can't seriously think Margaux would kill Celine for a plant," Dex said after we lost our giggles.

I shrugged. "People kill for less."

"But how valuable is a plant?" Dex asked.

"I don't know. Not much, monetarily, I don't think," I said. "But bragging rights. Auntie Akamai mentioned before that Celine wouldn't even share the Analise version of the plant with her own sister."

"Ah," said Dex. "Which is why Analise assumed her mother had taken some."

"It looked to me like more than one person took some," I said.

"Maybe even Analise," Dex said.

"Oh, well, it's named after her. But why would you think she would? Is there something I should know before I send her social requests?"

Dex shook his head. "No, no, nothing. She's good people." He started the Jeep, pulled a U-turn, and headed for Auntie Akamai's. "We should probably give Auntie Akamai an update."

I nodded. My phone dinged, and I looked down at it. "Oh, that's a bit creepy… We were just talking about her. It's Shannon of the Halloween-themed wedding."

"Oh, right. It's Monday night? On Halloween?" he said. "What are we going dressed as?"

"Well, at this point it needs to be something we can work out fairly quickly, since we haven't done any planning." I tapped my lip as I thought. "Humans who wear normal clothes would be easiest."

Dex chuckled and repeated *humans* like it was a tall order. "What did Shannon say?" he asked, nodding toward my phone.

"Oh, just telling me more details—you know, the when and where." I typed a quick response to her then clarified for Dex. "The Luau area at the resort." By then we had arrived home.

Home. Sometimes if felt weird to think of Auntie Akamai's as my home, but she had repeatedly insisted I should.

My father had hinted at wanting to know if I was coming home for the holidays. Growing up, we usually traveled on the Christmas holiday, and I didn't think they planned to suspend the tradition. Thanksgiving though, my mother went all out. Not that she cooked or baked, but she *directed* the creation of an amazing meal. I wouldn't mind going home for it. Besides, it was just a few days, and I could see the New England fall colors and the tree in Rockefeller Center. I needed to email my parents.

Dex followed me up the porch stairs and into the house. Auntie Akamai was in her chair, Paulie on the arm next to her, watching a singing competition on the TV. Judging by the box of tissues next to her, she was having a rough evening.

Maybe not the best time to accuse her good friend of the murder she was mourning.

Paulie turned his head and eyeballed Dex. "You stinky chicken," he squawked at him.

"You're the stinky chicken," Dex shot back.

"*Keiki*, stop arguing with the dang bird," Auntie Akamai said, her voice a flat monotone. She kept her eyes on the TV. "What have you guys been up to?"

Since she usually never asked, wanting to respect my privacy, I knew it meant her Auntie-sense was tingling. She glanced up at me with questioning eyebrows.

Dang it.

She waited, and I squirmed. *What did she know?*

"We found one of the cats from the shelter," I offered.

One of her eyebrows arched higher.

"Then he jumped out the car window and ran off. Near Celine's house. And we saw Analise," I said.

"Where did you find the cat? Or, should we say, where did the cat find you?" Auntie Akamai asked.

I shot a look at Dex. *Help me*. He was looking everywhere but at the two of us. It was like a swarm of bees was circling his head.

Well, he wasn't going to be helpful. It was painfully clear the tall ex-principal had called Auntie Akamai.

"We spotted the cat by Margaux's house," I admitted.

"Inside her yard?" Auntie Akamai asked.

"Well…no," I said, trying my best not to squirm. "After we came out of the yard."

"And," Auntie Akamai said, her eyebrows now level with her hairline, "what were you doing in Margaux's yard?"

I sighed then went and sat on the couch so I could face her at eye level. "Look, I know she's your friend. But the only thing Celine ate or drank that we don't know for sure what was in it, was her drink. Which Margaux made and which had muddled green leaves at the bottom." I held out a hand palm up. "Detective Ray mentioned digitalis, so we went to see if she had foxglove. And there are leaves missing."

Auntie Akamai's eyebrows took a nosedive. "So? Leaves fall off plants all the time. And I have foxglove about five feet away from the front door—are you going to go investigate those?" She pointed toward the front door.

"Okay," I said, holding my hands up. "But she also has a locked greenhouse with what looks very much like a cutting from Celine's bougainvillea inside. And Analise showed us the plant at Celine's, and I may not be an expert, but it was certainly missing branches. Based on Analise's reaction to it, several branches, in fact."

Auntie Akamai's face fell and her eyes began to tear up.

I glanced up at Dex and gave a chin nod toward the door. He nodded and was out of the house within seconds.

"It makes me so sad that people would steal her plant within days of her dying. That's just despicable!" She spat out the words.

"Analise was upset too," I said. "She focused on her mother, but who knows who took one."

"Was the bush destroyed?" Auntie Akamai asked.

I shook my head. "No, just, well, pruned unevenly, I guess you could say. Dex suggested someone took branches for her funeral."

Auntie Akamai dropped her head into her hand. "I'm sorry for snapping at you about Margaux. Those exact thoughts about the leaves in Celine's drink have crossed my mind too."

"It doesn't mean that's what happened," I said. "And you're right, the missing leaves could have gone anywhere." I remembered the other photos on my phone and pulled it out. "I took photos of some other plants out of curiosity. Do you know what these are?"

Auntie Akamai took my phone and slowly flipped through the photos. "Are these from Margaux's garden as well?"

I nodded. "What are they?"

"Rhododendron," she said, holding up the picture to me. Then she flipped to the next photo. "Hydrangea." She slid to another. "Oleander." She studied the final one before shaking her head. "I'd have to look this one up, but if it's what I think it is, it's worse than those others. Purple nightshade."

"What do you mean worse than the others?" I asked. "They're bad too? I've heard of the first three. They're everywhere in Washington State."

Auntie Akamai handed my phone back to me. "Bad as in poisonous. Every single one of them."

CHAPTER THIRTEEN

The rain pounding against the window woke me up Saturday morning, and of course, it was about ten minutes before my alarm was set to go off. I rolled over and checked the radar map on my phone. It didn't look like it was going to be stopping anytime soon. Doubtful we would be going on our dive in a few hours.

I slipped on a pair of distressed jeans and a lightweight sweater and headed out to see if Auntie Akamai had heard anything yet.

It looked like Auntie Akamai was thinking the same thing about the weather, standing on her back lanai, staring outside while she cradled her coffee. After getting my own mug, I joined her.

"Did the rain wake you, too?" I asked her.

She startled. "Oh, I didn't hear you over the sound of the rain," she said. "And no, it didn't wake me." She glanced at me, an odd look on her face. "I heard a weird noise."

"A weird noise? What kind of noise?"

"Like a wailing. A sorrowful, sad sound." She leaned forward and peered out the screen at the rain. "I haven't heard it since coming out here though."

"That's creepy," I said and shivered. There was a cool breeze, but not what I would consider enough to make me feel cold.

As if on cue, an inhuman cry filled the air. It sounded like it was coming from everywhere around us, even below. We both jumped and sloshed our coffees, and we ran for the door into the house. Auntie Akamai slammed the door behind us, and we stood staring at it.

"What in the world was that?" I gasped. "That was so scary!"

Auntie Akamai's eyes were huge. "That was much louder than before, too."

We stood and stared at the door but didn't hear it again.

"Maybe Dex can check it out?" I said hopefully.

"Or Kahiau." Auntie Akamai shook off the shock and headed for the counter. "Want some toast?"

"Sure," I said. "Have you heard from Kahiau about today's dive yet? The radar looked like it's around for a while." I sat at the table to check my phone again.

Auntie Akamai shook her head as she dropped some toast in her upright toaster, and then she joined me at the table. "My guess would be no dive. It's a little funny how tourists don't even consider it's the start of the rainy season."

I nodded. "They just assume it will be nicer here than wherever they are coming from. Which it probably is, just wet." I took a sip of my coffee. "I know it's not my business, but how does the business survive with all the rain cancellations?"

Auntie Akamai waved a hand. "It's not so many. But Kahiau will add some stargazing tours and whale-watching tours—on the good days, of course."

The wail started again, muffled now, and stretched out for a few incredibly long seconds. Auntie Akamai and I stared at each other.

I swallowed hard and decided to ignore it. "Oh, stargazing. That's cool! He did mention the whale tours a few weeks ago, but I hadn't heard of the stargazing yet." I stood to fetch the toast, butter, and jelly and brought them to the table.

I had just finished buttering my piece of toast when my phone buzzed, which made me jump a ridiculous amount. It was a message from Kahiau. He said the clients for the dive had canceled and asked me to do social media updates. I answered that of course I would and gave Auntie Akamai the update.

"So what shall we do instead?" She winked at me.

I raised my eyebrows as I sipped my coffee. "What did you have in mind?"

Auntie Akamai looked down at the table. "Well, I understand everything you told me last night and think I should probably talk to Margaux. I'm dreading it though." She sighed.

"Well," I said, tipping my head. "We could also ask the restaurant that made the food some questions."

Auntie Akamai frowned but nodded. "We should. Maybe we can go over for lunch. We have to find a way to address it. Just showing up will set Jennifer on edge."

"Jennifer? Oliana's daughter-in-law? Why?" I asked.

Auntie Akamai chuckled. "You think Oliana is prickly… Just wait 'til you meet Jennifer."

I thought back to the woman on the sidewalk after the gathering at Celine's house. "She was a tad negative."

Auntie Akamai snorted. "Negative. Yeah, that's a way to frame her personality."

"So we just need to be extra creative in the way we approach her," I said, dusting the toast crumbs off my fingers. "Speaking of creative, I also need to figure out costumes for Dex and me for the Halloween wedding."

My phone rang, interrupting any follow-up questions I had. I picked it up and stared at it. Who was calling me? I glanced up at Auntie Akamai's face, which mirrored mine with a confused look.

"Hello?" I said, putting the phone on speaker. "This is Kiki."

"Kiki?" a panicked voice came through the speaker. "This is Shannon. The Halloween bride."

"Oh, hi Shannon!" I glanced at Auntie Akamai and shrugged. It must be important for her to call me, especially this early on a Saturday.

"I need some help," she gasped. "I didn't know who to call."

"What's wrong?" I asked, sitting forward.

"The caterer fell through. They apparently double-booked by accident," Shannon wailed. "They can still do the cake, but there's no food. It was just supposed to be finger foods, but a lot of them."

"That's terrible," I said, unsure where she was going with this. "Were you working with Aloha Lagoon's wedding planner, Kristy Piper?"

"No, she already had two weddings. We've done this on our own, minus a photographer she referred us to. Do you know any caterers or restaurateurs?" Shannon asked. "Or anyone who can help?"

I looked at Auntie Akamai and gave a small raise of my shoulder. To my surprise, she nodded vigorously.

"Shannon, my landlady is with me. I think she has an idea. Auntie Akamai?" I slid the phone across the table, closer to her.

"Hello, sweetie." Auntie Akamai leaned toward the phone. "We know a family who run a restaurant. And if they can't help, I can always get my friends together and take care of you. Don't you worry."

"Oh, really?" Shannon sounded like she might sob. "You would do that for me?"

"Of course, dear," said Auntie Akamai. "Let us contact the restaurant, and we'll get back to you. Are you available to meet with them later today?"

"Yes," said Shannon. "Anytime."

"All right, Shannon, we'll call you back soon," I said after we got a few details about budget and timing. We disconnected.

I smiled at Auntie Akamai. "Two birds with one stone, perhaps?"

Her Cheshire cat grin told me she had been thinking the same thing.

* * *

Auntie Akamai said we needed to wait about an hour before we called Oliana, as she wasn't an early riser. So I grabbed a shower and got dressed while we waited. In the meantime, Auntie Akamai called Kahiau about coming over to look for the cause of the creepy sound. He agreed to come over, but not until later.

"He didn't sound very excited to help out," Auntie Akamai laughed.

We settled onto the couch to call Oliana. Auntie Akamai dialed the number and put the phone on speaker, holding it in front of herself.

Oliana answered with a grunt. "What?"

Auntie Akamai's eye rolled heavenward. "Good morning, Oli," she said cheerfully. "Kiki and I have a quick question for you."

"Mhm." Oliana sounded noncommittal.

Auntie Akamai nodded to me with her chin, encouraging me to speak next.

"Good morning, Mrs. Harris," I said. "There is this young couple who went diving with us who are having their wedding on Halloween, but their caterer fell through." I stopped, suddenly unsure what I was asking.

Auntie Akamai continued for me. "We were hoping you could give us an in with your son's restaurant."

Oliana sighed through the phone. "I have no idea what their schedule is, Akamai. You need to just call them." And the call went dead.

I stared at the phone. No wonder people didn't like her.

Auntie Akamai sighed. "And that there is my lifelong friend." She shook her head sadly. "She's gotten more grouchy as every year passes."

"Why?" I asked. I really wanted to know why Auntie Akamai stayed friends with her, but that was an inappropriate question.

Auntie Akamai shrugged. "I'm not sure. Just getting older and tired of life, I guess. She's had a rough go of it, losing her parents then husband so early."

"But she's only in her sixties, right?" I asked.

Auntie Akamai smiled. "We're getting up there, but we're not dead yet." A shadow passed over her face, and her smile melted away at her poor choice of words.

"Her health okay?" I asked.

"She's always been a bit sickly," Auntie Akamai admitted. "But nothing horrible." She focused on her phone again, looking up the number for Cain and Jennifer's restaurant.

"Lagoon World Café," a female voice greeted us. "How can I help you?"

"Jennifer?" Auntie Akamai said. "This is Akamai. We might have some business for you." She went on to explain Shannon's conundrum.

"Yes, I think we can help. Are you able to bring her down to discuss?" Jennifer asked.

We set a time for shortly before lunch so we could eat there as well. Or perhaps I should have said *eat lunch and investigate?*

CHAPTER FOURTEEN

I pulled Auntie Akamai's car to the curb in front of the restaurant. The rain had paused, but there was still no sign of the sun.

"The Premier Provider of World Fusion Cuisine," I read off the Lagoon World Café sign. "Is that a thing?" I asked. The name made more sense now, as before it sounded like a movie sequel or a theme park.

"According to Oliana, it means they can't cook one style food good enough to be the premier provider of one cuisine," Auntie Akamai chuckled. "I think they just don't want to settle on one."

"Well, fusion *is* a thing," I said. "Can't say if I've heard of world fusion, but it does make sense." I pulled my light raincoat closer around my body.

Auntie Akamai nodded. "He's quite a good chef. I'm not sure why she's not prouder."

"Why isn't she?" I asked. "Did she have other hopes for him?"

Auntie Akamai nodded. "She thought he should be a doctor. He's very smart, but it wasn't his interest."

"Wait," I said, holding up my hand. "Didn't Oliana want to go to medical school?"

Auntie Akamai nodded. "She did. Got into one and everything."

I tipped my head. "Why didn't she, then?"

Auntie Akamai smiled at me. "She wasn't as strong as you. Her parents had other plans for her, so she gave up her dreams to satisfy them."

"Strong…" I smiled. "More like stubborn and spoiled."

Auntie Akamai shook her head. "That's not how I see it. Or how Oliana does."

A shape appeared outside the window on Auntie Akamai's side, and we both jumped.

"Oh! It's Shannon," I said, giving the woman a wave. "The bride."

Auntie Akamai and I got out of the car, and we all hurried under the store overhang before I introduced the two women. Shannon was tall with jet black–dyed hair, and her fiancé, Tim, was oddly similar. Now that she wasn't involved in a water sport, she had makeup on—heavy black eyeliner and dark burgundy lipstick. Both were dressed in black. In short, they were pretty Goth, and now the Halloween wedding made perfect sense.

The couple's personality was far from what you might assume by their style. Shannon was bubbly, and her husband-to-be could best be described as gregarious.

Shannon threw her arms around me and squeezed the breath out of me.

"Oh, Kiki, I knew it was kismet to have met you!" Shannon squealed into my ear.

I patted her back gingerly. "Yes, it's wonderful," I gasped.

Shannon released me and grabbed Auntie Akamai next. Auntie Akamai enthusiastically accepted and returned the love.

Tim doled out hugs next, and then we finally went into the restaurant.

Behind a glass counter, a man and a woman stood facing each other. It looked like we had interrupted a heated discussion, but they immediately turned and plastered on big smiles. As Auntie Akamai was in the lead, I took a moment to check the place out.

In addition to the glass counter, there were a few two- and four-person tables spread around the room and right up to the plate glass windows on the front. Decoration was sparse and was mostly live plants (hopefully none of the poisonous ones), and a fake lei garland went around the border of the ceiling. They were the corner storefront, so there was a plate glass window to my right as well. And sitting at a table there, a schoolbook and notepaper in front of him, sat Noah.

I heard my name and turned to the couple as Auntie Akamai was introducing me.

"Kiki, this is Jennifer and Cain Harris, owners and operators of the Lagoon Café." Auntie Akamai had turned toward me, but her eyes darted to where I had been looking, so she saw Noah as well.

"Nice to meet you," I said, taking a few steps forward. "I'm so glad you might be able to help on such short notice."

Jennifer and Cain nodded and turned their attention back to Shannon and Tim, who were looking at the items in the case. I glanced down too and was surprised to see they had a section full of the same items Auntie Akamai had made, though their versions had a little more polish, with bloody stumps and painted nails. There were other things too, but the fingers caught my eye. I glanced at Auntie Akamai, who raised her eyebrow a millimeter then moved her eyes toward Noah.

I took the hint and wandered away, making a circuit of the room before I ended up in front of Noah's table.

"Hi, Noah. How are you doing?" I asked him with faux cheeriness.

He looked up at me then quickly away. His ears flushed red. "Homework," he muttered. He gestured at the notebook paper in front of him with algebraic formulas on it.

"Sorry to hear that. It does get better," I said. "Are you planning to go to college? I liked it because I could study more of what I was interested in there."

"I don't know," he said. He glanced over at his parents.

"What year are you?" I asked him.

"Listen, I don't want to be rude, but I'm kind of busy here," he said, gesturing at the papers in front of him and taking a quick look toward his parents.

I moved around behind him and bent over as if I was looking at his textbook but glanced toward the counter.

Jennifer was shooting daggers at me with her eyes.

I straightened. "Okay, doesn't look like anything I could help you with anyway," I said. "But please," I continued, "if there's anything I can help you with, or if there's anything you want to tell me…"

"Excuse me," Jennifer said, striding over. "My son is working on late work, and he's grounded anyway." She stopped, crossed her arms, and glared at me. She spoke again in a quieter and therefore slightly menacing voice. "You need to stay away from my son, Nancy Drew."

I stared at her. "What?"

"Oh, you know what I mean." Jennifer rolled her eyes. "Always getting involved in murder investigations. You think you're some young, hot Miss Marple or something." She took another step forward and gave me a thorough and very rude look from head to toe. "There is nothing for you to investigate here, missy."

"I asked him what homework he was doing," I said, crossing my arms as well. "People aren't allowed to be friendly to your son?"

Jennifer snorted. "Whatever. Just back off."

I looked toward the counter. "I brought you business, and you are being incredibly rude."

"You," she said, jabbing a finger toward my chest, "are being nosy."

I narrowed my eyes at her and leaned in. "Just so you are aware, if I was investigating something—which I am not—your behavior would put you at the top of my list." I tossed my hair. "So good job on not acting suspicious, lady." I turned halfway to Noah. "Good luck with your math." Then I marched out of the restaurant.

Since it had started drizzling again, I sat in the driver's seat of the car, leaning against the door and facing the restaurant. My arms crossed, I glared at the scene inside. I couldn't hear what was going on, of course, but it looked like Jennifer had switched gears in order to make the sale. When Shannon and Tim came out, they were smiling, despite the downpour. They gave me a cheery wave before they dashed off to their next appointment, laughing in the rain.

Auntie Akamai, on the other hand, looked concerned.

She groaned her way into the car. We both looked into the restaurant and could see that Jennifer and Cain had resumed the argument we had interrupted. Cain gestured toward Noah and then to me, and they noticed we were watching. Jennifer started to come out from behind the counter, but Cain grabbed her arm and held her back.

"Let's go before they come out," I said. "I'd rather not talk to her again." Plus, the rain was picking up.

"What happened?" Auntie Akamai asked after she had settled herself in the seat.

"I asked Noah about his homework, school, that kind of totally mundane thing." I stuck the key in the ignition and turned it. "She came over and accused me of acting like Nancy Drew and Miss Marple, warning me to stay away from her son."

Auntie Akamai's eyes went wide. "Did she threaten you?"

I shook my head before looking over my shoulder to check the street for oncoming cars. "No, but I told her we weren't investigating anything, but that if I *were*, the way she was acting would put her to the top of my list!"

"Oh, Kiki," Auntie Akamai said disapprovingly and then laughed.

I was about to pull away from the curb when a knock on the window made us both jump. It was Cain, leaning over in the rain, his hair already getting soaked and plastering itself to his head.

Auntie Akamai rolled the window down. "Yes, Cain?"

"I just wanted to say…um, thank you for the small plates ideas," he said.

"Small plates?" said Auntie Akamai.

"Appetizers," I said. I leaned forward. "Those are everywhere on the internet."

Cain nodded. "I know, but I hadn't thought of them until my mother mentioned what you served at the mahjong night."

Auntie Akamai shrugged. "Okay, then."

Cain hesitated. "I'm sorry about my wife, Kiki. She's very…upset." He went to glance over his shoulder then stopped himself. "She feels terrible about what happened to Celine, and we had the police here earlier. She initially refused to let them in, and they threatened to shut us down in order to search if we didn't agree."

"She doesn't understand that investigating is a process and refusing to help makes you look like a suspect?" I said sweetly.

"Oh, goodness," Auntie Akamai said. She shot me a look before turning back to Cain. "Why would they need to search here?"

He tipped his head and gave her a look. "The same reason they searched *your* kitchen, I would think," he said, his voice edging into sarcasm. "Anyway, I wanted to apologize for her rudeness. Noah said you just asked about school, so she overreacted."

"Sure," I said then gave a wave. "We have another appointment. Thanks for helping out Shannon and Tim." I put the car in Drive and waited for him to straighten up before I pulled away from the curb.

Once we were back on the road, Auntie Akamai chuckled. "Kiki, I like you more every day."

CHAPTER FIFTEEN

When we got back to the house, we were greeted by Kahiau sitting on one chair on the front porch and Paulie sitting on the back of the other chair. Kahiau stood and raised his hands in a shrug as we dashed through the rain to the porch.

"Didn't find your monster, sorry," he said.

"Monster?" said Auntie Akamai, coming to an abrupt stop.

"Monster!" Paulie screeched.

Kahiau pointed at Paulie. "Yup, your monster," he chuckled. "Though I think it's probably a cat, based on the prints under the back porch."

"A cat, Paulie." Auntie Akamai pointed at the parrot. "Not a monster."

"Monster," repeated Paulie stubbornly.

Akamai sighed and turned to me. "Perhaps that cat followed you home."

I frowned as I wiped some rain from my face. "I don't see how. It ran away near Margaux's house."

Kahiau stared at me. "How did it get to Margaux's? Did she adopt it?"

Oh. That hadn't occurred to me. "Maybe. We'll have to ask her," I said.

"Even if she did, how did it get here?" asked Auntie Akamai.

"Maybe it's a different cat," said Kahiau. "Weren't there more than a few unaccounted for?"

Auntie Akamai and I both nodded.

"It's still a good distance from the shelter though," added Auntie Akamai. She looked at her brother. "Coffee?"

He nodded, and we turned to go inside, but before we could get through the door, another car arrived and Detective Ray got out and hurried through the rain to the shelter of the porch.

"Ray, hello," called Auntie Akamai. "I was just about to put coffee on. Would you like to join us?"

"Yes, please," answered Detective Ray. "I could definitely use some caffeine."

Paulie glared at the policeman. "Monster," he muttered.

Detective Ray stopped short. "Did he just call me a monster?" he asked.

Auntie Akamai laughed then went back to pick up Paulie. "No, he's letting you know he thinks there's a monster under the house."

Detective Ray frowned. "Okay, that needs more explaining."

"We think it's a cat," said Kahiau. "Probably one from the shelter breakout yesterday."

"That's a bit of a trek," said Detective Ray. "But who knows."

We all removed our wet—and dirty, in Kahiau's case—shoes by the door. Auntie Akamai and I had house slippers, but the two men just followed us to the kitchen in their socks. They settled at the kitchen table while Auntie Akamai started the coffee. I pulled out the leftover finger cookies and an assortment of dips.

Both men stared at the finger shortbread cookie sticks.

Detective Ray pointed his own finger at the plate. "Are these the ones you served the other night?" he asked.

"Yes," said Auntie Akamai. "A wonderful way to see they're not poisonous, don't you think?"

Detective Ray looked at Kahiau. "You haven't upset your sister recently, have you?" he joked.

Kahiau laughed. "No, but I'd say she's probably upset at whoever she chopped the fingers off of!" He picked one up and tapped his chin with it like he was pondering who the victim was.

Detective Ray picked one up too. "They look like yours, Kiki."

I held up my hands to show I still had all of my digits. "Not mine."

I found myself staring at Detective Ray's usual Hawaiian shirt. I leaned closer for a better look. I'd thought it was normal but realized that the typical surfboards were being ridden by zombies.

Auntie Akamai brought the carafe of steaming Kona coffee to the table after delivering mugs, sugar, and cream. "Love the shirt, Ray," she said as she set down the carafe.

There was a lull in conversation while everyone got their coffees set up. Kahiau used a finger cookie to stir his cream into his coffee.

"So," said Auntie Akamai, "to what do we owe this visit?"

Detective Ray took a long sip from his coffee then set down his mug and rotated it a few times. "Well," he said and sighed. "I'm not getting anywhere with this investigation. Since you were here that night and have proven yourselves observant in the past…" He trailed off.

"You want to know if we've, um, observed anything?" Auntie Akamai asked. She looked at me. "Kiki?"

"We haven't been investigating or anything," I said, pulling a shank of hair forward to wind around my finger. "But yes, we have noticed a few things."

"Okay," said Detective Ray. He glanced at my hair winding between my fingers and waited patiently for me to go on. He knew my nervous tell.

I looked at Auntie Akamai. She frowned at her coffee but gave a slight nod.

Detective Ray noticed but didn't say anything.

"Okay, well, the only thing Celine ate or drank that wasn't something she picked—her dish from the restaurant—or we made," I said, gesturing at the finger cookies, "was her drink."

Detective Ray nodded. "The cocktail Margaux LaRoux made her."

"Yes," I said. "Her mojito. Which, as you probably know, comes with muddled mint leaves in it." I took a sip of my coffee. "So we were thinking, perhaps it wasn't *mint* in it."

The detective took a sip of his coffee. "I'm following. What leaf do you think it was?"

"Well, you mentioned there was a digoxin toxicity in her blood. And Auntie Akamai said foxglove flowers are really called digitalis."

Detective Ray nodded again. "And the leaves have the most toxicity."

I studied the detective. "So you already knew that."

He smiled. "But where did it lead you?"

I glanced quickly at Auntie Akamai. She was staring morosely into her mug, so I looked back at the detective. "Dex and I went into Margaux's garden and found some foxglove. It looked like some leaves had been recently removed." I pulled out my phone and showed him the photos of the picked-at plant.

Detective Ray looked carefully at the photo. I told him to look at the following photos too, and he slid through them.

"Several of those look familiar," he noted, tapping on the screen.

"Yes, they are common plants that are also poisonous," I said. "Rhododendron, hydrangea, and others."

Detective Ray had slid to the next photo and frowned at it. "What is this?" he asked, holding up my phone.

Auntie Akamai glanced up as well.

"Oh," I said, taking the phone from him. "That's a branch in a jar in Margaux's greenhouse."

"Why is the photo so bad?" Kahiau asked. "It's pretty unfocused."

"It was through the window and lit by a flashlight," I explained. "In person it was easier to see the blossoms. It's a branch of bougainvillea."

"Boo!" shrieked Paulie.

"I can see Dex was here," I muttered. "Yes, Paulie, boo-gainvillea."

Auntie Akamai rolled her eyes, and Kahiau and Ray laughed.

"Okay. And the significance of the boo-gainvillea is what?" Detective Ray asked. "Is it poisonous too?"

"I don't know about that, but we think it was from Celine's award-winning version, the one she named after her niece, Analise." I reached for a finger cookie and crunched it near its first joint.

"And?" Detective Ray asked. "What am I missing here?"

Auntie Akamai spoke up. "Celine wouldn't share that plant with anyone, not even Analise's mother. She was extremely proud of it but held it close. To her, it was very important and precious."

Detective Ray sat back and studied her. "But is it valuable enough to kill for?"

Paulie got bored with our conversation and flapped away to the living room.

Auntie Akamai watched him go then looked back at Detective Ray sadly. "I would say absolutely not, but I'm not a plant nut." She gazed back at her mug and rotated it a few times before continuing. "I have known these women for years. I cannot see any of them killing over a plant."

Detective Ray watched her until she looked back up at him. "Do you see any motive outside of this plant for someone to have wanted to cause Celine harm?"

Auntie Akamai shook her head. "No, I can't think of anything. I have no idea why anyone would want to hurt Celine."

Detective Ray nodded. "I agree," he said. "Which is a problem. Without a motive…" He raised his hands in surrender. "But there's another thing," Detective Ray said. He gestured at my phone. "You saw leaves removed from Margaux's foxglove plant."

I nodded. "Yes?"

"That was us. The police. With Margaux's permission, we tested the plant against the substance found in Celine's blood. It doesn't match," Detective Ray said.

Auntie Akamai and I looked at each other.

"So Margaux's foxglove didn't kill Celine?" Auntie Akamai let out a breath she must've been holding for days. "Oh thank goodness."

I frowned. *So why did he let me go on yapping about it?*

"The substance in her blood was digitalis itself—not the plant, but the medication," said Detective Ray solemnly.

Auntie Akamai gasped. Her hand flew to her throat, and her face visibly paled.

I leaned forward and took her other hand. "What is it, Auntie?"

Auntie Akamai didn't respond. She just looked at Detective Ray with wide eyes.

"It looks like you are aware of a source of digitalis," Detective Ray said quietly.

Auntie Akamai nodded, her eyes filling.

Kahiau looked from face to face. "Akamai. What do you know?"

Detective Ray didn't wait for her to answer. "Oliana Harris is prescribed digitalis."

CHAPTER SIXTEEN

"Wait a second," I said. "Why did you ask about the foxglove plant if you already knew it wasn't the substance in her blood?"

Detective Ray held up a finger. "I didn't ask you about the plant. I asked you if you had observed anything." He gave a small smile. "I just didn't stop you from talking about it. I was wondering where your observation led you."

Auntie Akamai sniffled. "You don't think Oliana killed Celine, do you?"

Detective Ray studied her. "I don't have evidence to suggest she did or that she didn't. We are getting a warrant to search her house, and she's coming in this afternoon for an interview."

Auntie Akamai shook her head vigorously. "There's no way. The three of us have been friends since birth, pretty much. There's just no way, Ray."

Detective Ray leaned back and clasped his hands on his comfortably ample belly. "We have to check."

Auntie Akamai straightened suddenly. "What about Stella? Have you looked into her?"

"Stella Keawe? Your next-door neighbor, *Stella*," said Kahiau.

Detective Ray tipped his head to the side. "I've met her. She seems very…"

"Gossipy?" I offered.

The detective smiled. "I was going for *knowledgeable*." He made air quote to emphasize his sarcasm.

"Euphemism," I muttered, reaching for another finger. I picked off the almond-sliver fingernail and popped it into my mouth.

Detective Ray chuckled and leaned forward, elbows on the table. "Akamai, why do you suspect Stella?"

"She has been jealous of our friendship for decades," Auntie Akamai said, waving a hand. "But more recently, she was upset we chose Margaux to replace the fourth in our mahjong group, which makes it awkward when we hold it at my house."

"Has she ever said or done anything that makes you think she would hurt Celine?" Detective Ray asked.

I held my cookie finger up. "She did say weird things to me at mahjong at the senior center," I said. "She implied there was something in the EpiPen. And when I asked her who would put something in Celine's EpiPen, she said if she said the name, she would be the next victim."

Auntie Akamai looked at me. "You didn't tell me that!"

I shrugged. "I forgot. It seems like she says bizarre things for attention." I turned to Detective Ray. "But could there be anything to it? Could there have been something in or on her EpiPen?"

Detective Ray pursed his lips. "If there was, that would mean Celine was killed by someone who knows their way around an EpiPen as well as had access to hers."

"Or swapped it out," said Kahiau.

"Who brought it out?" I asked. "I remember Margaux administering it, but I don't remember where it came from."

Auntie Akamai cringed when we all looked at her. "Oliana got it out of Celine's purse."

"So back to Oliana Harris," said Detective Ray.

I thought back to that night and to Oliana's almost complete lack of emotion. "Oliana was pretty calm during the emergency and wasn't exactly broken up after the ambulance took Celine away," I said. "I do remember afterward, she said something like it should have been her."

Auntie Akamai's frown deepened. "I remember now. I thought she was saying since her health is worse. You don't think she meant it was literally supposed to be her, do you?"

I stared into her dark-brown eyes. "Like she knew it was coming?" I asked. "That it was meant to be her?"

"Well…" Kahiau cleared his throat and gave me a meaningful look.

"What, Kahiau?" asked Auntie Akamai.

"Well, if there's not a motive to purposely kill Celine, maybe it was an accident?" Kahiau said. "Maybe Oliana was right, and it was *supposed to be* her?"

"Accident or not, if Celine was poisoned, it's still involuntary manslaughter," said Detective Ray. "A death caused by an unlawful act. Which typically has a reason to be done."

"I think what Kahiau's getting at," I said, "is maybe the intended target was someone else? And somehow, Celine was poisoned instead."

"Combined with the other theory..." Detective Ray said. "Oliana knew she was being targeted, but the poisoner accidentally killed Celine."

"Which would make the EpiPen a nonissue, since that being tampered with would not only be deliberate, but specifically targeting Celine," I said. "But if there is something to it being accidental, motive is still an issue."

"If Oliana knew someone was trying to poison her, a motive would be self-preservation," Auntie Akamai pointed out.

"Could she have swapped the dishes of food?" Detective Ray asked. "Known hers was poisoned and switched with Celine?"

"We went over all of it when we thought Celine had an allergic reaction," Auntie Akamai said. "Each of us had our own dishes we usually ordered. Everyone got their specific meal."

"And Kiki got her worms." Detective Ray nodded. "We found remnants of each dinner in the garbage."

I sat up straight. "Did you find the digitalis?"

"It's still at the lab," Detective Ray said. "And everything was pretty much mixed together, so it might be hard to figure out what is what."

"Sorry," I said. "I had no idea the garbage would become murder case evidence."

Detective Ray opened his mouth to answer but was interrupted by the inhuman wail we had heard earlier.

"Oh, wow!" said Kahiau. "I can see why you called me to check that out! That is creepy!"

"Do you really think that's a cat making that noise?" I asked.

"I have no idea, but I've heard they can make some pretty bizarre sounds," said Kahiau.

Paulie seemed to agree, flying back into the kitchen and landing on Auntie Akamai's shoulder. "Monster!" he screamed into her ear.

"Oh, for goodness' sake, Paulie!" Auntie Akamai covered her ear. "Shush, will you?"

The creepy cry continued, and Detective Ray looked toward the back door. "Maybe let it in?"

"Monster," crooned Paulie. Then he fixed a beady eye on Detective Ray and clicked his beak menacingly.

Detective Ray stared back at him. "I think he's threatening me."

"Arrest him, please," muttered Auntie Akamai. "A menace to society."

"Well," said Detective Ray, wiping his hands together. "Is there anything else we should discuss?"

"I have a question," I said. "The creepy animal sound reminded me. I know it's not your department, so to speak, but have you heard anything about why Noah Harris released all those animals at the shelter?"

He shook his head. "Yeah, not my area. Looks like a kid acting out like they sometimes do."

"The timing seems weird," Auntie Akamai said. "He was apparently close to Celine, as we've seen him very upset about her death." Auntie Akamai pointed to me and back at herself.

Detective Ray nodded. He pulled a small notebook from the pocket of his pants and a removed a pencil stub from the spiral at the top. He flipped it open and made a note. "Okay," he said. "I'll check in on Noah Harris, Stella Keawe, the EpiPen, and the monster under your porch." He grinned and closed the notebook. "Just kidding about that last one." He turned to Auntie Akamai. "Thank you for the coffee, Akamai."

She held out a hand to retain him for a moment longer. "Can you look at Jennifer and Cain Harris as well? See if they had anything to gain by Celine or Oliana dying?"

He nodded. "I'll look into the bougainvillea as well." He reopened the small notebook and added those thoughts. Then he stood, and I walked to the front door with him.

"Kiki," he said when we stopped in front of the door. "Promise me you'll come to me if you hear anything. Don't get yourself into trouble."

I nodded. "Of course!" I waved a hand to shoo away his worries. "I don't need another scar."

Detective Ray's shoulders slumped, and he shook his head. "Just be careful," he said before dashing through the rain to his car.

When I got back to the kitchen, Auntie Akamai and her brother were standing side by side looking out the window on the kitchen door.

"What's going on?" I asked, peering between their shoulders.

"I think we should let the cat onto the porch," said Kahiau. "Then you'll be able to capture it and take it to the shelter."

Auntie Akamai frowned. "I don't want it going after Paulie." She turned to me. "What do you think?"

I tipped my head back and forth a few times while I considered. "Maybe just the porch so the cat can get out of the rain," I suggested. I turned to Paulie, sitting on the back of a chair at the table. "What do you think, Paulie? Should we let the monster onto the porch?"

Paulie tipped his head and stared at me. "Monster," he muttered. Then he fluffed up his feathers and began grooming.

I turned back to Auntie Akamai. "Looks like he doesn't mind."

Behind my back, Paulie made a raspberry sound.

Chuckling, Auntie Akamai opened and held the door for me to make my way past her into the screened-in porch. She closed the door to the kitchen firmly behind me.

I paused, waiting for the wailing sound, but it was quiet. I pushed the screen door wide open and gazed outside. Her backyard was basically the beach, a stretch of sandy grass turning into only sand, stretching to the shore. The big banyan tree to my right half hid the screened shack I used to live in. Basically a cement pad with walls of screen and a roof, it was originally my own little apartment.

Since the rain had slowed to a drizzle, I sat on the top step, halfway on the porch and halfway out. "Here kitty-kitty-kitty," I called softly. "Is that you, Loki?"

I waited for a few minutes until the drizzle built up enough on my legs that I decided I had enough. I stood and went back to the kitchen door and turned the knob. I paused when I heard a voice from inside.

"Akamai," said the voice through the window, "if I'm going down for this, I'm taking you with me!"

CHAPTER SEVENTEEN

Auntie Akamai was standing by the kitchen counter, looking like she was lucky to still have a grip on the coffee carafe in her hand, while Oliana Harris sat at the kitchen table, looking imperious and fierce.

"Auntie Akamai," I said. I wasn't sure what to follow with, so I looked at her guest. "Mrs. Harris. It's nice to see you."

"Your face says different," she growled. She turned back to Auntie Akamai. "As I was saying, if I have to go in to the police station to talk to that detective today, you need to go with me. You have experience with him." She pounded her fist on the table. "If I'm going, you're coming too!"

"I'm not sure Detective Ray would let me sit with you, Oli. I've already spoken with him," Auntie Akamai said. "I think he prefers to talk to people one on one." She glanced at me as if for help.

"Yes," I offered. "He likes to speak to sus—people separately." I hoped she hadn't caught my original thought.

But of course she had.

"Suspect? I'm no suspect, young lady!" Oliana fumed, shaking her tight gray curls.

Auntie Akamai's eyes pleaded with me, so I sat at the table and looked Oliana straight in the eye as if to say *I'm not scared of you.* "Actually, you are. That's why you're being questioned," I said. "And if I understood correctly, he's getting a warrant to search your house."

Oliana's mouth fell open, and she looked from me to Auntie Akamai and back. She closed her mouth and opened it again, as if she were doing an impersonation of a fish. "That is the most ridiculous thing I have ever heard!" she sputtered. "Why?"

"They're trying to find out what happened to Celine, Oli," Auntie Akamai said soothingly.

"I had nothing to do with it!" screeched Oli. "Why would they ever think I did?"

"Because she was poisoned with a digoxin, the same chemical as the medication that you take," I said, leveling my gaze at her.

"What?" gasped Oliana. Her hand flew to her throat. "She was poisoned? Not a heart attack after an allergic reaction?"

I held a finger up. "If I remember right, you had suggested that is what happened, in a way. She may have been given something to give her an allergic reaction, and perhaps her EpiPen had the substance, like Stella had theorized. Regardless, they're not done running tests, so they're not sure yet how exactly she was poisoned."

Auntie Akamai came to the table and poured Oliana a mugful of coffee. "Decaf," she said.

Oliana frowned up at her. "Thank you for remembering." She glared at the cup for a moment then took a sip. "I should only have one cup of coffee a day because of my heart," she explained to me. "And I hate it."

"We should address the possibility of Oliana being framed," I said to the women. "If you didn't do this but it looks like you did, perhaps there's a reason it does."

Auntie Akamai picked up on what I was doing. "Yes," she said. "Can you think of anything, any advantage to you?"

"Like what," Oliana growled.

"Is there any financial gain for you if she passed?" I asked. "Or something to do with her garden?"

Oliana sipped her coffee and pondered. "I can only think of reasons to knock *me* off," she said, laughing sarcastically.

A little light bulb went off in my head. "Like what?" I asked.

"Inheritance, of course," Oliana sniped at me, like I was dense.

"Who inherits what?" I pressed.

"Well, my oldest son already runs the pineapple plantation, but he would inherit it," she said with a shrug.

"And your second son, Cain, what would he inherit?" Auntie Akamai asked.

"A lump sum. But the plantation is worth considerably more," Oliana said, taking another leisurely sip.

Auntie Akamai took a little intake of breath and made eye contact with me. She turned to Oliana. "And your older son is sick."

Oliana squeezed her eyes shut and nodded. "Yes. Cancer. He's not doing well." She took a shaky breath and shook her head.

I looked between the two women. "So if your older son passes, the younger gets the pineapple business?"

Auntie Akamai's eyes went wide, and then she shook her head. "What would that have to do with Celine though?" she asked.

"I'm just spitballing here," I started, and then after seeing the older women's faces, I thought about a different way to phrase that. "This is a theory," I said. "If Oliana were to be convicted of murder and go to jail, and if her son were to pass away, then Cain inherits."

Auntie Akamai pursed her lips. "That's a bunch of ifs."

Oliana nodded but did a mini fist pump. "Jennifer," she said. "I could easily see Cain's wife being devious."

I couldn't help but *not* be surprised. "She is a bit, um, confrontational."

"She's a—" started Oliana.

"Oli!" interrupted Auntie Akamai. "Peaceful thoughts, remember?"

Oliana snorted then stood to put her mug in the sink. She glanced out the kitchen door window as she passed and stopped abruptly. "Why, pray tell, is there a gargoyle on your lanai, Akamai?"

"A gargoyle?" said Auntie Akamai, chuckling. She joined Oliana at the window. "Ah," she said. "He is a bit gargoyle-y." She waved a hand at me to join them.

I went to stand with them and peeked out the window. A gray cat sat there primly, his tail wrapped neatly around his body, ending at a curl around his feet. His fur was wet and muddy in places, giving him the look of being made of cement.

"Oh," I said. "The poor baby!"

Auntie Akamai chuckled. "You can use one of the old towels from the bottom of the linen closet." She turned to Oliana. "Well, let's go talk to the detective and leave the gargoyle to the girl."

"Gargoyle?" Paulie repeated, flapping his way into the kitchen. He landed on the back of a chair. His pronunciation wasn't clear with the unfamiliar word, and it basically sounded like *guh-goyle.*

A moment later, I heard the front door close as the women left for the police station.

"Don't scare the kitty!" I pointed a finger at Paulie accusingly. "Be nice!"

"Kitty," repeated Paulie. He clicked his beak and looked at me with his creepy eyeball.

I hurried to the linen closet and grabbed two of the old towels from the bottom shelf then hurried back to the kitchen. I set one of the towels on the table and shook out the other.

"Be nice," I repeated to Paulie before going to the door and peeking out the window again.

The gargoyle was still there and in the same position, which gave me the fleeting thought that perhaps it was actually a cement statue.

I opened the door a crack and poked my head out. "Hello, kitty. Don't be afraid."

The cat—Loki, I was sure—cocked his head and watched me as I slid out the door and kneeled a few feet from him.

I held the towel out. "Want me to dry you off?"

Surprisingly, the cat made a little *brow* sound and calmly walked toward me. I reached out with a corner of the towel, and he walked into it, rubbing his face against it as he came closer.

This cat was so chill.

I studied him as I wiped some of the mud off. I was 99.9% sure this was the same cat as the night at Margaux's garden and Loki from the shelter. Just muddy.

"Loki," I said. "Is that your name?"

The cat sat still and let me rub him, but I was just making the towel muddy. "You can't clean the mud off yourself," I said to the cat. "It would be icky to lick. I think I need to bathe you."

I reached out and gently dropped the towel over the cat then picked him up. I carried him through the door and to the kitchen sink, lowering him into it. He stood in the sink and looked around. I made sure to warm the water first then moved slowly, washing the mud off and using a little dish soap for the worst bits, making sure to rinse him completely. He either didn't care or understood what I was doing. Perhaps his previous owner had bathed him.

"Okay, buddy, almost done. I thought cats didn't like water!" I spoke quietly in a singsongy voice. The cat, for his part, sat calmly, as if he understood I was helping him.

I felt a draft of air as Paulie flew to the countertop to investigate. He edged toward us and his pupils pinpointed when he saw the cat, but he very wisely kept his beak shut.

As for the cat, he watched the parrot with interest but seemed more into his bath than acting like Sylvester seeing Tweety Bird.

When I was done, I sat on the couch with him on my lap and dried him with the clean towel. When he was as dry as he could be, he curled up on my lap and, purring, went to sleep. Paulie had followed me to the living room and sat on Auntie Akamai's chair back, keeping a watchful eye on us.

"Guh-goyle," he muttered.

My phone buzzed.

How did it go with the gargoyle? Auntie Akamai asked.

I sent a picture back of the clean and fluffy cat curled up on my lap. *Bathed and dried*, I answered.

Shall I pick up food and a litter box? she asked, followed by a winky face.

I sent back a gif of a woman jumping up and down saying *Really?!*

Auntie Akamai sent back an eye roll emoji and a blowing a kiss emoji. She had really stepped up her emoji game since I moved in with her.

How is Oliana? I asked.

Don't know. They won't let me in. I'm at the café, she texted back. We were frequent visitors to the café across the street to the police station. *I drove her though, so I'll be a while.*

I sent a thumbs-up, put down my phone, and went back to stroking the cat's soft fur. A moment later, my phone buzzed again, but this time it was Dex.

Thought of a costume for us, he texted.

Oh, good. I hadn't spent much, if any, brainpower on that issue yet. *What?*

In lieu of answering, he sent a selfie of himself and a very big brown dog. From the angle of the photo, I could tell it was a very tall dog. The background looked like the NASH Animal Shelter we were at the previous day.

What is THAT? I asked.

A Great Dane! he texted back. *Isn't he cool!*

I knew Dex wanted a dog…but a Great Dane? Wow.

Yes, he is. What is the costume? A cowboy and a horse?

Dex sent a laughing emoji, and then my phone rang.

"Remember what you told me the restaurant lady called you?" Dex asked me.

"A nosy something or other," I said then laughed. "She said a young, hot Miss Marple."

"Right. So I started thinking about other detectives, one with a man too so we could do a couple costume. And who has a big, brown dog?" Dex giggled gleefully.

I was busy internally squeeing over him saying a couple costume when I realized. "Scooby-Doo!"

"Yes! I'll be Fred, and you can be Daphne, and this dude will be Scooby!" Dex's enthusiasm was contagious.

Since Dex was nowhere near blond and I wasn't a redhead, it would require wigs and a little clothes shopping, but it sounded like a great idea. Which I told him. I did have one question though.

"Whose dog is that, and are you borrowing him?" I asked.

"Well…" Dex said, drawing the word out, somehow, into a complete sentence.

"Because…" I said and then texted him a photo of the gargoyle sitting on my lap.

CHAPTER EIGHTEEN

Dex and I had never talked about that next huge step—living together. We sort of skirted around the subject. I thought he was thinking the new apartment that he had his sights on was for both of us, though he hadn't said it out loud.

Just like I hadn't said out loud yet that I wanted to invite him home with me on Thanksgiving. I did need to float the idea to my parents first anyway.

But now, with him thinking about adopting a huge dog and me possibly taking in the furry gargoyle, cohabitating could be a problem.

But it was a problem we would have to deal with later.

"That explains the paw prints in the back of the Jeep," said Dex. "He must've hitched a ride from the shelter and then gotten back in the Jeep when we were talking to Analise. He did run in that direction."

"Smart cat," I said.

"Determined cat," Dex corrected. "He fell in love with you. I'd hitch a ride to be near you too," he said with a smile in his voice.

"Aww, Dex," I said, warmth flooding my body.

"Well, I think we can wait a while to introduce our boys. I mean, nothing's official yet with either of them," he backpedaled. "Oh! How's he doing with Paulie?"

"So far, ignoring him. Paulie is keeping an eye on him and is staying unusually quiet," I said, looking over at the parrot. He was pretending to sleep but had a beady eye on the cat. At least the pupil I could see wasn't tiny anymore, which I assumed was a good thing. "Oliana was here when the cat came to the porch, and she called him a gargoyle, so that's what Paulie calls him. Sort of."

"What was Oliana doing there?" Dex asked.

"She was called in to talk to Detective Ray and wanted Auntie Akamai to go with her."

Dex grunted for some unseen reason. "What's the theory now?"

"Well," I said, stroking the cat's fur, "Oliana's theory now is that someone is trying to frame her. She suspects her son, Cain, and his wife, Jennifer, want her incarcerated so they can take over the pineapple plantation and have her fortune."

"Naw," said Dex. "Cain loves being a chef. He wouldn't want to run a business instead of cooking." There was another grunt. "Ooof, this guy thinks he's a lapdog." There was the sound of a struggle as he attempted to remove the dog.

"Did you know Oliana's oldest son is sick? Terminally ill. So Cain may not have much of a choice if they want the business to stay in the family," I said.

"Yeah, I heard. It's rough," said Dex. "I still think that's pretty ridiculous. Cain doesn't want the company."

"Maybe not," I said, remembering how Oliana disparaged her daughter-in-law, "but maybe Jennifer does."

"Hmm. Well, are you hungry?" Dex asked. "No, not you, dog. You're probably always hungry. I'm talking to my beautiful girlfriend."

I smiled. "This cat is probably hungry too, though it appears more tired than anything else."

"Do you want to get dinner?" Dex asked me. "Dang, he knows that word too," he said, laughing. "Why don't I turn this guy back in to his room and head on over to get you? I know just the place for dinner."

"I'm not sure what to do with the cat," I said. "I don't think I can just leave it in the house. What if it needs the bathroom?"

My problem was solved before the words were out of my mouth. Auntie Akamai opened and peeked in the front door and looked around. Seeing me on the couch with the furry gargoyle on my lap, she covered her mouth, hiding a smile.

She pushed the door farther open and pulled in her wheeled shopping bag. She strained to get it over the doorjamb then closed the door behind her. Leaving the bag by the door, she tiptoed over to gaze at the cat.

She shot a look at Paulie before grinning and mouthing, *I always wanted a cat.*

I waved her closer. "He's sleeping. Go ahead and pet him."

She ran a hand down and around the curl of his body. "So soft."

I smiled up at her. "I think he's exhausted. But Dex wants to take me to dinner, and I don't know what to do with him."

Auntie Akamai waved a hand toward the front door. "I bought him a box and kitty litter. We can set him up in your room and close the door. How has *he* done with him?" she whispered, holding up her hand to hide her finger pointing at Paulie.

"Really good, actually," I said. "The cat completely ignores the bird, and the bird watches him like a hawk. Or a parrot, I guess." I laughed.

I stood, lifting the cat into my arms. He remained limp and sleepy, so I carried him into the bedroom and set him on the bed near the pillow. He stood, made a circle, and then curled up in a tight ball and went back to sleep.

I helped Auntie Akamai take the things from the shopping cart and set up the corner of my room with the litter box. She got two small bowls, filled one with water and the other with cat kibble, and put those on the other side of the room.

"Okay," she said, straightening. "Now I think it's safe to leave him in here. I need to get back to Oliana, and you need to get to dinner with Dex." She looked at the cat again. "Once we know you two get along, we won't have to keep you closed up in here," she told the cat.

We left the room, and I closed the door softly behind me, turning to find a stern-looking parrot on the floor blocking our way.

"Oooo, I think you upset him now, Auntie," I whispered.

Paulie glared at Auntie Akamai then strutted back and forth like a father who had just caught his daughter sneaking in after curfew. If he could've crossed his wings, he would have.

"Guh-doyle," he said to Auntie Akamai. When she didn't respond, he stopped and bobbed his head forward. "Guh-doyle!" he screeched. The first syllable sounded like he was being strangled, or gargling, so perhaps it was his way of saying the cat made him feel sick. Why he added a D to the word, I had no idea.

Auntie Akamai reached down to pick him up, but he snapped his beak at her.

"Geesh," she said, straightening. "I guess we know how he feels about the cat. But what is he saying?"

"Gargoyle, I think?" I suggested. "What Oliana called the cat when she saw it."

"Guh-doyle," repeated Paulie. "Bad birdie." He sneezed as if to emphasize his displeasure.

There was a quiet knock on the front door, and Dex stuck his head in. After greeting us both, he turned to me. "Ready?"

I grabbed my purse from the hook by the door, and the three of us went out.

"*Guh-doyle!*" screamed Paulie from inside.

"What?" laughed Dex. "He is sure mad about something. The cat, I'm guessing?"

Auntie Akamai nodded. "Yes, he's acting like a brat, but he'll adjust." She kissed us both on our cheeks. "Where are you headed?"

Dex gave a mischievous grin. "I believe I'm in the mood for some 'world fusion' food. What do you think, Kiki?"

* * *

We sat at the corner table next to the one where Noah had been earlier. The counter staff was different than this morning, with Jennifer Harris nowhere in sight. Cain Harris was still in the kitchen though, and he delivered our food himself.

After setting down our dishes, he gestured to the third chair. "May I?" he asked.

"Of course," Dex said.

"I figure you're here to talk to me anyway," Cain said quietly as he slid into the chair. He nodded toward me.

"You work a long day," I said.

He shrugged. "I come and go. We are open for breakfast and again for dinner. We only do cold foods for lunch."

"Jennifer works mornings?" I asked, pulling my braid forward to fiddle with it.

Cain nodded. "I couldn't exactly talk in front of Jennifer. She's very…sensitive."

Again, not how I would describe her.

"What is she sensitive about?" Dex asked after a longing glance at his plate holding a sushi burrito.

"She's very protective of my son, Noah," he said.

I spread my napkin on my lap. "What does he need protecting from?" I asked.

"Everything," Cain said, shaking his head. "Girls, tough teachers, criticism…"

"Like things Oliana says to him?" I asked quietly.

Cain shook his head, looking at the table. "She's hard on him. She's hard on me." He sighed and looked up. "I have never felt like I'm good enough, and I guess it transferred to Noah."

"Why do you think she feels you're not good enough?" I asked.

"Because my passion lies in there," he said, gesturing back at his kitchen. "Not in what she wanted me to do."

"What's that?" Dex asked before his hand darted forward and he grabbed an errant edamame bean and slipped it into his mouth.

"A doctor," said Cain. "She wanted me to go into medicine." He shook his head in disgust. "She never pushed my brother to do anything other than take over the business."

"I wonder if that's what he wanted to do," I murmured.

"Probably not," Cain admitted. "And I imagine he's felt a lot of pressure to take it over, but he seems satisfied with his—or her, really—choice."

"It's odd she'd push you to do something other than your passion, when exactly that happened to her," I said.

Both men looked at me.

"What?" asked Dex.

"Oliana wanted to be a doctor, but her family wasn't supportive," I said. "She had to take over the family business."

"What are you talking about?" asked Cain. "Where did you get that from?"

I stared at him. "She told me," I said slowly. "You didn't know?"

Cain shook his head slowly. "No, she isn't into sharing hopes and dreams with me."

"It was probably the way she was raised," I said, my own mother in mind. "Women didn't have much choice but to obey their families. Even now, it's hard."

Dex gave me a sympathetic smile and reached for my hand.

Cain looked down at the table again. "It does cast a new light on things with her."

I leaned toward him. "You should sit down and have a talk with her."

Cain gave a sarcastic cackle. "Right. Like that's ever going to happen on Jennifer's watch."

CHAPTER NINETEEN

"Okay," said Dex. "No offense, but I'm not sure I've ever heard you say anything nice about your wife."

Cain cringed. "No, it's not like that."

Dex raised his eyebrows. "I'm serious," he said. "I really haven't."

Cain slumped into the seat and studied his hands like a dermatologist looking at a suspicious mole. "She was an amazing woman when I met her. Such a lifesaver after my first wife died. She saved me, made me whole again." A smiled played his lips. "And was such a blessing for Noah."

"But then?" I prompted. He needed to spill before my Naan poke-pizza got cold. Or should I say *colder*.

"What started as a comfortable mothering has turned into stifling and obsessive overprotectiveness," Cain admitted.

"Especially of Noah," I said.

Cain nodded.

"She became a Smother," joked Dex. When we gave him blank looks, he spelled it out for us. "A s-mother. A smother mother."

Cain just stared at Dex.

Dex shifted uncomfortably and cleared his throat then charged on. "And especially of Noah's potential inheritance, I'm guessing," Dex said, less of a "guess" than a statement.

Cain sighed again, which was an answer enough. He glanced over at the shop door as it opened and two couples came in. He watched as the hostess greeted and sat them.

"I can see you'll need to go in a minute," I said, "but can I ask about the night Celine died? Was there anything strange that happened in the kitchen? With the food?"

Cain faced us again and hesitated. He folded his hands and placed them against his lips, his fingertips blocking his nostrils.

I shook off the hope he washed his hands before cooking again and waited.

Finally, he nodded. "There was something one of my dishwashers said. Let me send him out." He stood. "I need to get ready for those customer orders."

Dex nodded. "Thanks, man. We appreciate it."

After Cain walked away, he looked down at his plate and wasted no time grabbing his burrito and taking a huge bite.

Wrapped tightly in white paper to keep the seaweed "tortilla" from tearing, the burrito was filled with strips of vegetables and salmon, surrounded by sushi rice. Unfortunately for Dex, his enthusiasm had him eating some of the paper as well.

I followed his lead and picked up my Naan bread pizza, topped with Poke bowl toppings of avocado, crunchy edamame, crispy onion, and marinated chicken. I wasn't a fan of raw fish, so I had ordered chicken as my protein. A little blob of wasabi was on the side, but I avoided it.

Our plates were bare before a young man came around the counter and approached us.

"Hey, man," he said to Dex. "Chef said you wanted to talk to me?" He gave me a quick once-over and a nod.

Dex gestured at the chair. "Actually, my girlfriend had a few questions."

The young man sat in the chair and directed his attention to me but struggled to keep his eyes off the low neckline of my sweater. I wished I had brought my raincoat with me.

"I'm Kiki," I said.

"Jorge," he said.

"Okay, I was wondering if you saw anything weird on Tuesday night, especially related to a delivery order Noah took around six o'clock." I self-consciously moved my braid around to the front, though it wouldn't cover much. In fact, it made him look again.

Jorge shook his head. "Naw. The weird thing I saw was earlier in the day." He looked at Dex expectantly.

Dex raised his eyebrows and stared back at him.

After a short silent standoff, Jorge looked back at me. "I saw the sous chef talking with a woman out by the dumpsters. She handed him a bottle and left."

"What kind of bottle?" Dex asked.

Jorge held up his hands about six inches apart. "'Bout this big. Dark. Couldn't see through it."

"What did the woman look like?" I asked.

Jorge looked at me. "The sous chef or the other woman?"

I closed my eyes for a moment. "The woman who gave the sous chef the bottle."

"Oh. Older lady, but real hip-looking," Jorge said. "Black lady with an afro and great arms. Kinda hot for an old lady."

Margaux.

I glanced at Dex and saw he was frowning.

"She gave the sous chef a bottle," I repeated.

Jorge nodded and glanced at Dex again. "That all?"

Dex nodded. "Yeah, man. *Mahalo*."

"*Mahalo*," Jorge replied as he stood. "I'll take your plates if you're done."

We both nodded. As he reached down to pick them up, Dex slid a twenty-dollar bill toward his plate. Jorge casually pocketed it before he sauntered away with the dishes.

"That's not good," Dex said, stating the obvious.

Before we could discuss, the hostess approached us with the check and two small plates.

"Dessert on the house," she said without ceremony as she clanked them down in front of us.

"Awesome," said Dex enthusiastically, pulling a dish filled with what looked like *haupia*, a Hawaiian coconut pudding, toward him. Apparently, the huge sushi burrito didn't fill him up.

I pulled mine toward me but only ate half, leaving the rest for Dex. We didn't talk until we were done. We left the money for the bill on the table and walked out into the night.

It was finally clear of rain, and the temperature was perfect. Once outside, I grabbed his hand.

"Let's walk a little," I suggested.

Dex rubbed his belly. "I'm not sure I can walk," he laughed. Then he sobered and looked down at me. "Margaux," he said.

I nodded. "That's not good."

"Understatement," said Dex.

"Detective Ray sounded like he had ruled Margaux out." I hooked my arm through his. "But this does tell us there was probably something in the food that wasn't supposed to be there."

"But Margaux?" Dex shook his head in dismay. "I can't even imagine it."

"We need to talk to the sous chef," I said. "Like right away."

"I agree," said Dex.

"And Jennifer," I added.

Dex frowned. "I might leave that one up to you."

I laughed. "Wimp."

Dex squeezed my hand. "I think you may not want to mention this to my aunt."

I shivered, and Dex noticed.

"Cold?" he asked me. He pulled me toward a bench overlooking the beach, and we sat. He wrapped an arm around me an in attempt to keep me warm, though I wasn't sure the shiver was from the cold.

We sat and watched the sky darken over the ocean.

"Do you think we'll dive tomorrow?" I asked.

Dex nodded. "I think so."

"Kiki?" a woman's voice spoke behind me.

We turned to see Jennifer standing behind us.

"Hi Jennifer. How are you?" I asked.

Cain's wife looked a little worse for wear this evening. "Tired," she said. "And not in the mood for this, but I think we need to have a little talk."

Dex started to pull back from me, but I clamped a hand on to his leg.

"You're welcome to sit," I said, pointing at the other end of the bench. "What's up?"

Jennifer stared out at the sea. "I'm sorry for being so abrupt with you this morning. I'm just worried about Noah. I'm concerned you've set your sights on him as responsible for Celine's allergic reaction."

Abrupt? I almost laughed, but instead I watched her face. "It wasn't an allergic reaction, Jennifer. Celine was poisoned."

Her mouth dropped open before she clamped a hand over it. "*What?*"

I nodded. "I don't think they know how exactly yet, but there could have been something in the food." I held up a hand. "That's not why I was interested in talking to him though. I don't suspect him."

"You don't?" Jennifer said.

"No. He seems really broken up about it, like he really cared about Celine. I doubt he'd do anything to harm her," I said.

"He wouldn't," she said, placing a hand over her heart. "He is devastated. He is convinced he did something wrong and feels very guilty, though he shouldn't."

"He has no motive for Celine dying," I said. "But…"

Jennifer's head snapped to look at me. "What?"

"Oliana. What does he stand to gain when she passes?" I asked and prepared for an explosion.

"Goodness, we all stand to gain from that old bat dying," Jennifer snorted.

"The pineapple business and fortune, obviously," I prompted.

Jennifer nodded. "Cain's brother is driving the business to the ground. I mean, thank goodness people always want pineapple. But I have an MBA! He only has an inheritance. I'm more qualified."

"But what about Cain?" I asked. "Doesn't he want to keep the restaurant?"

She nodded. "Of course. But if we had the capital, he could open a larger, fancier one, out there on the property. He could be a five-star restaurant instead of a beachside storefront," she scoffed, waving a hand in the direction of the restaurant.

I nodded and waited for her to go on. It felt like she was just getting started.

"Not to mention we need to provide for Noah. College, if he wants, and an inheritance. The kid deserves it." She crossed her arms. "Oliana hates the poor kid. Never has anything nice to say to him."

"Is he the only one in that generation?" I asked. "Does Cain's brother have kids?" I leaned toward her. "What is his name, by the way? Please don't say Abel."

We both laughed.

"No, it's Nathan, after his *legendary* father," she said scathingly. "And no, he doesn't have kids. I mean, there might be a few little Nathans running around out there. The guy's a player." She turned her face away and muttered what sounded like, "Not unlike his father."

"So, Noah is the only heir," I said.

She turned back to me and nodded. "Only *official* one. He'll inherit it all."

CHAPTER TWENTY

After our conversation with Jennifer, who thanked me for bringing the wedding party job to them before leaving, we headed back to the house.

"What do you think she meant by only official heir?" I asked Dex.

Dex raised a shoulder. "My guess is she suspects an illegitimate kid running around out there."

I looked out the side window as I pondered that. "So Jennifer might be worried her brother-in-law has a kid who could take his father's place—and inheritance—from Noah."

"I'm not sure how it would be motive for anyone killing Celine—or Oliana, for that matter," said Dex. "I'm sure it's worrisome to Jennifer, but wouldn't it simply be speeding up the inheritance process?"

"Yeah. It's interesting and all, but I don't see how it could be connected."

"Looks like Oliana is still at the police station," said Dex, pointing. "Her car is still here."

Sure enough, as we pulled up to Auntie Akamai's house, we had to park next to Oliana's sleek Mercedes. Once we got into the house, we saw we hadn't made quite the right deduction.

Auntie Akamai and Oliana were sitting in the living room, watching *Jeopardy*. Paulie sat on his perch near the window, which was unusual when Auntie Akamai was home and especially when she was in her chair.

"Paulie still pouting?" I asked in lieu of a hello.

Paulie muttered something from his perch, and Auntie Akamai laughed. She pointed at Oliana.

Shock of shocks; on Oliana's lap was the gray cat, curled up and looking very much like he belonged there.

"He looks comfortable!" I said, laughing. I went and sat next to Oliana. "How was the police station?" I asked her.

She waved a hand. "Fine, it was fine. No problem."

I looked at Auntie Akamai, and she tipped her head toward her shoulder.

"Well, that's good," I said, sitting back. I glanced over at Dex and raised an eyebrow, but he shook his head. I ignored his unspoken advice and turned back to Oliana. "I know you're probably tired of questions, but can I ask you one more?"

Oliana closed her eyes. "For you, yes, I can answer a question."

I felt a completely unnecessary trill of joy. *Aww, for me?*

"I was wondering if you knew of Nathan having any children?" I said and held my breath.

Oliana's eyes flew open, and she turned to me so quickly she disturbed the cat.

"*Nathan?*" she blurted.

"I think Kiki means Nathan Junior, not Nash," Auntie Akamai smoothly interjected. She glanced at me. "Her son as opposed to her husband?"

"Oh," said Oliana, leaning back into the couch cushion again.

The cat stood, stretched into a perfect impersonation of a classic Halloween cat, and then looked at me. He stepped gracefully across her lap and into mine, where he sat and stared at my face.

"No, I don't know if Nathan Junior has any kids," Oliana answered.

"Okay," I said, my attention now on the cat. I rubbed his ears, and he rubbed his cheeks on my hands. He began purring and, after more petting, settled down onto my lap.

"That's it?" asked Oliana.

I nodded.

"Do I want to know why you asked that?" Oliana asked.

"Just wondering about Noah, if he's basically the only heir to the pineapple plantation," I said. "I don't think it can be any kind of motive to make sure he inherits if he's the only heir."

Oliana grunted then pushed herself to a stand. Auntie Akamai stood too.

"Dex," said Auntie Akamai, "can you drive Oliana home? Kiki and I will follow in my car to bring you back to your Jeep."

Oliana put a hand on Dex's arm. "I don't like driving at night anymore."

Dex nodded down at her. "No problem."

Oliana reached up and grabbed his cheek. "Such a cutie." As they walked for the door, she made a show of looking at his backside.

"Don't you be grabbing those cheeks, you old bat," chided Auntie Akamai, and Oliana tittered. "Those are for Kiki only."

My goodness. I felt the heat rise in my own cheeks, and Auntie Akamai poked my shoulder as we walked.

"Let me put the cat in the bedroom so Paulie doesn't murder him while we're gone," I said, diverting to the bedroom.

Auntie Akamai was facing the parrot when I came back into the living room. "That little beast said *murder* in the creepy voice after you walked out. Putting the cat in there was probably a good idea."

Dex walked with Oliana on his arm to the passenger side of the Mercedes. She handed him the keys, and he opened the door for her. Once she was settled, he shut the door and turned to me.

I blew him a kiss and got into the driver's seat of Auntie Akamai's car.

"What?" said Auntie Akamai as she slammed shut her own door behind her. "You're not going to close my door for me?"

"Oh, sorry." I started the engine and looked over at her.

She was smiling and waved a hand.

"The cat seemed pretty darn comfortable on Oliana," I said as I reversed into the road to follow Dex.

"We probably should name him," said Auntie Akamai. "Unless you were going to keep calling him Loki."

I shook my head. "The woman at the shelter said it means flower, and that's not a good name for a male cat."

"I think the skunk in *Bambi* was a boy, but that's beside the point," said Auntie Akamai. "Oliana and I thought of a name to suggest to you."

"What?" I asked.

"It came from Paulie, actually. His pronunciation of gargoyle sounds like *guh-doyle*," said Auntie Akamai. "So how about Doyle?"

"It doesn't mean anything in Hawaiian?" I asked.

She shook her head. "Nope." She turned to me. "What was with that question, for real?" she asked.

I kept my eyes on the road. I didn't necessarily like driving at night either. "We talked to Cain at the restaurant—he called his brother Nathan, by the way. Nothing too interesting there. But then Jennifer approached us outside the restaurant."

"Uh-oh." Auntie Akamai chuckled. "That couldn't have been good."

"No," I said, "it was okay. She actually apologized for her previous behavior, which was a surprise." I slowed to a stop at a stop sign.

"Did Dex just run the stop sign?" Auntie Akamai said, leaning forward.

"I don't know," I said. "It's hard to tell, but he doesn't always come to a complete stop."

"But in Oliana's fancy car..." Auntie Akamai tutted. "Anyway. Back to Jennifer."

"Right," I said. "I was asking her the same only heir question, and she said Cain's brother was a player and might have done some running around...and I think she said like his father."

"Hmm," said Auntie Akamai. "Odd. Oliana's never said anything about that. Where does Jennifer get off saying that?"

"I don't know. I figured you'd know if there was anything to it," I said.

The taillights of the Mercedes had long disappeared into the night. I hadn't realized I drove so slowly compared to Dex.

"If someone else could stake a claim when Nathan Junior passes, it would be a problem for Noah, but none of that makes sense for being motive to murder Celine or to set Oliana up for her murder." I edged the old car up to speed as we entered the highway. Oliana's place was farther out, past the edge of town. "Don't you think?" I asked Auntie Akamai.

I turned a little to look at her, and at the same time, she threw herself against the window.

"Stop!" she shouted. "Go back!"

I hit the brakes. "What?" I shouted back.

"Someone went off the edge of the road. Go back!" Auntie Akamai said urgently, turning and looking out the back on her side.

I checked the road behind me, but it was dark. I put the car in Reverse and slowly crawled backwards along the shoulder until Auntie Akamai told me to stop. She jumped out of the car as I put the car in Park and pushed the button for the hazard lights and then got out my side and trotted around.

I heard Auntie Akamai's gasp before I got to her side, where she stood looking down into a ditch.

Then I gasped too.

The nose of Oliana's Mercedes was buried in the ditch, half underwater, while the tires still spun.

CHAPTER TWENTY-ONE

"Call 9-1-1," Auntie Akamai said before she started down into the ditch.

"Wait, Auntie. You call, and I'll go down." I was clutching my phone, so I turned on the flashlight and looked at the terrain to get into the ditch.

The edge was steep and muddy from all the rain. I immediately slipped and ended up traversing down on my backside.

"Are you okay?" Auntie Akamai called out to me.

"Yes," I yelled back. *Muddy but okay*. I wiped my phone off on my sweater and inched my way toward the car. I could hear Auntie Akamai talking on the phone behind me but no voices from the car.

"Dex! Oliana!" I shouted. "Can you hear me? Are you okay?"

I got close enough to have my hand on the trunk of the car and was relieved the tires had stopped spinning.

"*Dex?*" I shouted again as I edged my way along the side of the car. The farther I moved toward the front of the car, the deeper the water got. It was to my knees now and was moving by from behind.

I got to the window and looked in. Both occupants looked like they were slumped over asleep, Dex leaning toward Oliana in the passenger's seat. I banged on the window. "Dex! Dex!" I tried the door handle, but it was locked—must've been one of those cars that locked automatically when you started driving. Usually, I would think that was a good thing, especially for an older woman driving a flashy car, but right now, not so good.

I banged and shouted a few more times and finally saw Dex move. His hand went to his head, and he looked around groggily then sat more upright. Due to the position of the car, he was still leaning to the right.

He looked in my direction, and I saw his mouth move.

"Turn off the car!" I shouted through the window.

His hand moved to the ignition area, and the engine stopped. He felt along the door, trying to find the lock, or perhaps the window.

I pointed at Oliana. "Is she okay?" I shouted through the window.

Dex turned, like he was surprised someone else was sitting there. He picked up his phone from the cup holder, leaned toward her, and held the phone screen under her nose. After what felt like hours, he turned back and gave me a thumbs-up.

I turned and shouted up to Auntie Akamai that they were okay. Her free hand flew to her heart.

The water in the ditch was blocked by the car and slowly rising around my legs. I realized with a start it was above my knees now. Dex went to open the door, but I waved a hand and shook my head.

"Just stay there," I said close to the window. "I don't know what will happen with the water." I pointed at the ground.

Dex pressed his forehead against the window to look at the ground, and that's when I saw the blood on the right side on his head.

I pointed to my own head, to the same area that was bleeding on him. "Are you okay?"

He raised a hand and touched his head gingerly then nodded.

Behind me, I heard sirens. I looked up the slope to where Auntie Akamai was standing, but she was now facing the road, waving her arms above her head. Moments later, the sirens stopped as the flashing vehicles pulled to the side and parked. Auntie Akamai directed the emergency workers down into the ditch. The first one who arrived told me to return to my vehicle.

I slogged up the side of the ditch, assisted by one of the firemen going down, and flopped to the ground once I got to the road.

"Are you hurt?" a paramedic stopped briefly to ask.

I shook my head and pointed down the slope. "My boyfriend, Dex Kekoa, and Oliana Harris are in the car. His head is bleeding, and I couldn't see her, but he said she was breathing."

The paramedic nodded, and then she and her partner went back to the ambulance. After a moment, they passed again with a backboard.

I stood, and Auntie Akamai and I leaned against the trunk of her car and waited.

A uniformed police officer was dropping flares onto the road and then came over to us and pulled out a notebook. "Can you tell me anything about the accident?" he asked.

"It's Oliana Harris," said Auntie Akamai, "and my nephew Dex Kekoa. He was driving her home because she doesn't like driving in the dark, and we were following to get him home after."

"Had he been drinking?" the officer asked.

"No, of course not!" Auntie Akamai seemed to grow a foot taller in her indignation. "He's a good boy! And why the heck would I have him drive my friend if he had?"

The officer, chastised, simply nodded. "Any idea why they went off the road?" He looked around the ground briefly. "It's not too wet, so I can't imagine it was a skid."

"I don't know," Auntie Akamai said. "They were too far ahead of us. We didn't actually see it happen."

"He's awake," I said. "He hit his head, but he might remember."

The officer glared at me. "You went down there?"

"Yes," I said. "But I wouldn't let him open the car door." I turned to Auntie Akamai. "I was worried the car would fill with water." I turned back to the police officer. "He didn't try moving her. He just made sure she was breathing."

"Kiki? Akamai?" a familiar voice spoke behind us, making all three of us turn.

"Detective Kahoalani. What brings you by?" the officer asked.

"I was driving home," Detective Ray said. "I recognized Akamai's car. Is everything okay?" he asked Auntie Akamai.

She shook her head, her former bravado for the uniformed police officer quickly becoming tears. She pointed down the slope, and Detective Ray leaned around us to look.

"It's Oliana and Dex," I said, tearing up as well. I couldn't take seeing Auntie Akamai tear up, and the adrenaline was wearing off.

"*What?*" Detective Ray said. "How? Are they okay?"

"Dex was driving Oliana home because she doesn't like driving in the dark. We don't know why, but they went off the road." Auntie Akamai dabbed at her eyes. "We almost drove right by!"

"Dex seems okay," I added. "But Oliana was still unconscious when I came back up. Dex is a good driver, Detective

Ray." I shot a dirty look at the uniformed officer. "And he hadn't had anything to drink."

Detective Ray frowned then turned to the uniformed officer. "Tell the tow truck that pulls it out to bring it to the station. We'll need to look at it."

The police officer hesitated.

"There is an ongoing murder investigation involving Oliana Harris," Detective Ray said testily. "We'll need to check out that car."

Just then, Dex appeared at the top of the slope, assisted by a fireman. The fireman led him past us to the ambulance, where he sat him down.

The police officer hesitated, looking at Detective Ray, who nodded toward Dex. The officer turned to go question Dex.

I took a step in his direction too, but Detective Ray held out his hand and gave a quick shake of his head.

"Have you called Oliana's family?" he asked.

Auntie Akamai shook her head. "Not yet. I didn't want to worry them without having a status report. I know I would hate to get half information."

The three of us stood shoulder to shoulder and gazed down at the Mercedes and the emergency workers who were on the passenger side of the car.

"Please be okay," Auntie Akamai whispered.

CHAPTER TWENTY-TWO

I shifted yet again in the uncomfortable waiting room chair, seeking a position that wouldn't make my bum go numb. It was an impossible wish.

"What is taking so long!" moaned Auntie Akamai. It seemed like hours had passed since they told us they would be taking Dex for X-rays on his arm. He had already gotten stitches on his temple.

Kahiau and Dex's mother, Sarah, entered the waiting room at a run. "Akamai!"

Sarah grabbed Akamai's hands while she listened to the most recent news: Dex was fine, minus a head laceration and possible broken arm. Then she turned to me and grabbed me into a hug.

"Oh, Kiki!" Sarah cried into my ear.

"He's okay, he's okay," I assured her, rubbing her back. "But they had to shave part of his head for the stitches."

Sarah pulled back, her dark eyes wide, but she smiled. "Oh, he's probably very upset about that. Thank you for putting it into perspective for me." Her eyes were the same as Dex's, which made my eyes sting with tears. "It's just hair, and it will grow back. He's hurt but will heal."

Kahiau shook his head with amusement then turned back to Auntie Akamai. "I'm so glad you saw them in the ditch. Who knows how long they would have been there!"

Sarah refocused her attentions onto Auntie Akamai, and Kahiau turned to me. "Was the road slick or something?" he asked me in a low voice.

I shook my head. "It didn't seem like it to me, but maybe there was something on the road or something ran out in front of him and he swerved. I have no idea."

Kahiau sighed and dragged a hand down his face. "And how is Oliana?"

I looked at Auntie Akamai, who was being strangled with Sarah's relief and unable to answer, so I looked back at Kahiau. "She's in serious condition. Her family hasn't arrived yet."

As if on cue, a crowd of bickering adults entered the waiting room.

Bickering being a euphemism.

Jennifer Harris interrupted her dressing down of Oliana's sons when she spotted me. She made a beeline for me, momentarily pausing the argument between her husband, Cain, and an older and thinner version of Cain who I assumed was his brother, Nathan.

"Why are you here?" Jennifer blurted, bearing down on me.

I took a step back, and Kahiau stepped forward to shield me.

"There was an accident," he said soothingly.

"Yeah, but was it?" snapped Cain. "Where's our mother?"

"You should ask at the desk," I squeaked, pointing around Kahiau to the nurse behind the counter.

Nathan Junior turned and went to the desk, but Cain and Jennifer were looking for a fight and fired hostile questions at us. *Why was Dex driving her car? How did the accident happen? Why did Dex steal her car and run over her? Why was Kiki trying to kill Oliana?*

Auntie Akamai stuck her fingers in her mouth and let loose an earsplitting whistle that made my ears ring. "People," she shouted, holding up her hands. "Calm down. It was a car accident! No one is at fault!"

"If it was an accident," said Jennifer sarcastically, "why was Dex driving?"

"What?" Dex's mom, Sarah, said. "That doesn't even make sense."

I opened my mouth to add Dex was driving Oliana so she wouldn't get into an accident. But smartly closed my mouth again. *Wait... Did she say why am* I *trying to kill Oliana?*

"Why would I do anything to hurt Oliana? I barely know her!" I sputtered.

The nurse from the desk approached us, Oliana's older son in tow. "Harris family, please come with me."

Jennifer pointed at me. "I'm not done with you yet!" she spat before turning on her heel and stomping after the men.

"Oh yes, you are!" shouted Auntie Akamai at her retreating back. She spun around to her own family. "The nerve of that woman."

Dex's mom put her arm protectively around me. "Why was she making accusations about Kiki? That doesn't even make sense!"

"Thank you, Sarah," I mumbled. "I would never do anything to hurt either one of them, but especially Dex."

"I know, sweetheart," Sarah said, hugging me again. "The woman is crazy. Don't worry about her."

"Why would she even say something like that?" Kahiau wondered out loud to himself. Then, as it dawned on him, his eyebrows rose. "Wait a second."

"Maybe we should go check on Dex," said Auntie Akamai, grabbing Sarah's arm and trying to tug her away.

Sarah was watching her husband's face. "Wait," she said to Auntie Akamai, and she reached out a hand to stop her. She turned to Kahiau. "What is it?"

Kahiau pointed at Auntie Akamai and me. "They have been investigating Celine's murder."

Sarah looked at us. "And Dex?"

I nodded. "Yes."

Which earned me something a girl never wants to see from her boyfriend's mother.

That look.

"It was his idea," I mumbled, looking at the waiting room carpet. It was a disgusting green and burgundy. "He wanted to go to dinner, I didn't know where until we were there."

"You went to *their* restaurant to question *them*?" Kahiau asked, pointing in the direction the Harrises had gone. "What exactly was the point of that?"

"We did find something out," I said.

"Something to do with Celine's poisoning?" Kahiau said.

I nodded. *But I can't say it in front of Auntie Akamai.* "But also, there might be more heirs to Oliana's fortune."

"More heirs?" Sarah asked and then chuckled. "Heirs sounds so old-fashioned."

"Jennifer implied there might be more, so we were assuming she was talking about her brother-in-law," I said, "but based on Oliana's reaction, I'm wondering if perhaps it is someone in an earlier generation."

I could feel Auntie Akamai staring at me. "Go back a second. What are you not telling me?" she asked. "And why?"

I turned and gazed into her eyes. I gave a quick shake of my head. "What do you mean?" I asked lamely.

Auntie Akamai's lips went thin. "You said something having to do with the poisoning but didn't mention anything about that before."

I gave her a pleading look. "We were going to check into it before bringing it up."

"Just say it," Auntie Akamai said.

I looked at the ugly carpet again. "The dishwasher saw Margaux give a small, dark bottle to the sous chef." I glanced up at Auntie Akamai when she didn't respond.

She was frozen.

"We weren't going to throw Margaux under the bus or anything. We were going to ask her about it instead of just telling Detective Ray," I said.

Auntie Akamai's eyes darted over my shoulder.

"Tell Detective Ray what?" asked…Detective Ray.

I turned slowly to see the detective standing there, watching me.

"Oh," I said.

He waited for me to respond for a long, long moment before turning to Auntie Akamai. "How are Dex and Oliana?"

"Dex is okay, but getting an X-ray on his arm," Auntie Akamai said. "But Oliana is more seriously injured. I don't have a recent update on her." She paused for a breath. "Her family is here."

Though they were simple words, she layered them with meaning.

Detective Ray nodded. "I'll see if I can talk to them." He paused and looked at me. "But first, come over here and talk to me."

Cringe.

I followed him to the other side of the waiting room.

"What is it?" he asked me.

I repeated the story about the small, dark bottle exchanging hands on the sly behind the restaurant.

Detective Ray nodded. "Okay," he said. "That's it?"

I frowned. "Yes."

"Nothing about the accident?" he asked.

I shook my head. "No. Why?"

"Well, we have no evidence of motive to kill Celine, but now the theory about Celine being accidentally poisoned instead of Oliana has more credence," Detective Ray said. "There's more possible motives to cause harm to Oliana, as well as concrete evidence pointing to her being the object of malice."

It took a moment for what he said to sink in.

"Concrete evidence?" I asked.

Detective Ray tipped his head to the side. "Perhaps a poor choice of words."

"Huh?" I frowned.

"Preliminary findings in looking at Oliana's car," he said, "are the brakes were disabled."

CHAPTER TWENTY-THREE

"Disabled?" I stared at Detective Ray. "What exactly does that mean? Like cut?"

He nodded. "I'd like to keep this quiet for now, so lower your voice please." He glanced over my shoulder at the others. "And I know you'll tell Akamai, but keep it to just her, okay?"

I nodded, still stunned. "So the investigation is now about Oliana?" I asked.

He nodded. "Do you have any insights to share?"

My mind was on spin cycle. "I'm sorry, I can't think straight right now."

He reached out a hand to pat my shoulder. "It's okay. You know where I am if you need anything." He turned and looked toward the desk nurse. "I should probably go check on Oliana—and her family."

I held up a hand to pause him. "There is something weird. Jennifer and Cain Harris were spewing all kinds of garbage about Dex or me causing this accident on purpose."

"You?" Detective Ray tipped his head to the side, and my mind superimposed Paulie's tipped head over his. "You weren't even there."

"I know. That's why it's weird," I said.

"I'd say interesting, actually." Detective Ray raised his eyebrows. "Sometimes guilty people will project their guilt on others."

He gave me one last nod and headed for the nurse's station.

I went back to Auntie Akamai and her family. They gave me some odd looks, but I was bailed out of answering questions by the arrival of Dex's doctor.

"Mr. and Mrs. Kekoa?" The doctor made a slight bow to Kahiau and Sarah. "Your son is doing fine, but he does have a broken clavicle as well as a break in his arm." To emphasize, the doctor pointed at his collarbone and patted his forearm. "His head wound required a couple of stitches. We're watching him for signs of concussion, so we will keep him overnight for observation."

"Can we see him?" Sarah asked.

The doctor nodded. "I can take his parents back, but everyone else," he said with a slight head incline at Auntie Akamai and me, "will have to wait."

"Can you tell me anything about Oliana Harris?" Auntie Akamai asked, stopping the doctor.

"She's stable and out of danger at the moment. It is touch and go for someone her age," the doctor said before leading away the Kekoas.

Sarah gave my hand a squeeze before following the doctor. "I'll let him know you're here," she whispered.

After they were out of earshot, Auntie Akamai grunted. "Someone her age…" she muttered before plopping down into a chair. She glanced up at me and patted the seat of the chair next to her.

After I reluctantly joined her, she leaned over and whispered, "So, what did Ray have to say?"

I hugged one of my arms across my body and buried my face in my free hand. "It's not good." I peeked at her between my fingers. "Not good at all."

Auntie Akamai glared at me. "All right. I hear you. It's not good. Tell me."

I dropped the hand by my face and hugged the other arm. "It wasn't an accident," I said.

Auntie Akamai's jaw headed for the floor. "*What?*"

"Someone tampered with Oliana's car," I said. "Which leads Detective Ray to believe Oliana was the original intended victim. Celine somehow got caught in the crossfire, if you will."

"And Dex now, too," fumed Auntie Akamai. She turned to me, her eyes flashing. "We have to figure out who this cretin is before anyone else gets hurt!"

"I agree," I said. "We need to start over from scratch and see who would want Oliana dead."

Since we couldn't do anything further at the hospital, we headed home. Our plan was to go over the motives list we had made when we thought Celine was the intended victim and see if any applied to Oliana.

And see how Paulie and the newly named Doyle were doing.

There were no clumps of fur or feathers on the floor, so it looked like they had done fine, which we would expect since they had a door between them. They were separately very happy to see us, and Doyle didn't want me to put him down, so I sat at the kitchen table with him on my lap.

Auntie Akamai plonked a mug of herbal tea down in front of me. I couldn't help the face I made, and I failed to hide it.

Auntie Akamai sat down and gave me an exasperated look. "It's not going to kill you—or keep you up when it's time to sleep." She pushed honey across the table to me after dribbling some into her own.

"I don't think either of us are going to get much sleep anyhow," I said but placated her by taking a tiny sip of what I referred to as "stick and twig water."

Auntie Akamai gripped a bright-pink pen in her hand and looked down at the list. "Clearly, Oliana would not have mistakenly poisoned herself and then cut her own brakes lines. I doubt she even knows where brake lines are." Auntie Akamai paused, pen poised over the paper. "I don't even know anything about brakes, other than they need fluids." She looked up at the ceiling. "Or at least used to," she muttered.

"So, next?" I asked, nudging her back to our task.

She looked at her page. "Margaux."

I stared into my mug, pondering. "I don't know. I just don't know why she would kill anyone, to be honest."

Auntie Akamai began making the circles in the margin again, pink bubbles mixed in with the previous black ink ones. "I agree." She shook her head. "As they say, she has no dog in the fight. Whatever the fight might be."

"Okay. So, Oliana's family. Her sons, Nathan Junior and Cain, her daughter-in-law Jennifer," I said. "And Noah."

"Noah?" Auntie Akamai looked up from her bubble-work. "You can't think that boy has killed anyone!"

"What if his displays of emotion are based in guilt?" I said. "They seemed a little extreme."

Auntie Akamai stared at me, so I backpedaled. "Maybe he was manipulated or used by someone else."

"Like perhaps his parents." Auntie Akamai pointed her pen at me. She clearly was warming to the idea.

I leaned forward and put my elbows on the table. "Let's go over their motives. They have the most."

"Inheritance." Auntie Akamai underlined the word twice on her paper. "That's all it comes down to."

I nodded. "Maybe… The only issue with *that* is they are going to get it anyway." I held up one finger. "Nathan Junior is terminally ill." I raised a second. "And he has no heirs."

"They're impatient. They don't want to wait for nature to take its course." Auntie Akamai shook her head in disgust. "I don't feel like we're old, but it's not like it's going to be decades and decades!"

"Maybe they need money now?" I suggested, absently stroking the sleeping cat curled up on my lap. "Perhaps the World Fusion Café is not doing well. Jennifer did mention wanting to use the pineapple plantation buildings to make a fancier restaurant. Maybe the café is on the verge of failure?" I paused, thinking. "Or the pineapple company?"

Auntie Akamai tipped her head as she looked at me. "Why would you say that?"

"Jennifer said Nathan Junior was running the company into the ground. Maybe she wants to save it so Noah will have his legacy." I took another sip of the earthy tea. "She says she has an MBA and is more qualified than Nathan to run a company."

Auntie Akamai's eyebrows shot up. "And yet she can't keep a café in business?"

"Exactly," I said. "But who do we ask about those businesses?"

"You've already gotten one version from Jennifer," Auntie Akamai said. "I think it's time to talk to Nathan Junior."

"I agree. Both about the businesses and whether or not Junior has Juniors." I took another sip of the tea and smiled at Auntie Akamai. "I think I'm actually starting to like this stuff."

CHAPTER TWENTY-FOUR

The dang cat kept me up half the night with him wanting to play, which was cute…at first. Now he was all lovey, rubbing his whiskers on my check and trying to lick my hair. Finally, he settled down at the end of the bed, pretty much when it was time to get up.

I checked my phone to find a text from Kahiau.

Dex doing ok. Coming home today. No dive due to family emergency.

I texted back. *Ok. Give him my love. And hugs to you guys too.*

I decided since there was no going back to sleep now, I would call New York and talk to my parents. My mother answered on the first ring.

"Katherine!" she trilled from thousands of miles away. "How are you, dear?"

This seemed like an auspicious start.

"Hello, Mother. I'm good. How are you and Dad?" I asked.

"Oh, wonderful, dear. We were just talking about you, weren't we?" my mother said back.

I could hear my father agree in the background, and then my mother switched to speaker and I could hear him more clearly.

"How's the diving?" he asked.

"It's great, when we do it. This is the start of the rainy season, apparently," I said.

"I don't imagine it's cold though?" my mother asked.

"No, it doesn't feel like autumn here," I agreed. "That's sort of one of the reasons I was calling…"

There was a drawn-out pause on the other end, and I could picture them looking at each other. Hopefully with hope in their eyes.

"It feels very much like autumn here," my mother said carefully. "The colors are especially nice this year."

"Yes, I've seen the pictures you both keep sending," I said. "They're amazing…and they make me want to come home. To visit, I mean."

"Oh, we would love to have you come home," my father said quickly.

I could hear a little arm smack and a hiss from my mother.

"We mean, if you want. We don't want to pressure you," amended my father.

"Well," I said, "I would like to come home for Thanksgiving. Would that be okay?" Before they could answer, I hurried on. "Christmas is the high season here, of course, so I don't know if coming home at Christmas would be possible."

"Thanksgiving would be wonderful, Kiki," my dad said, his deep voice rich with unusual emotion.

"Yes, dear, Thanksgiving would be wonderful. We rather thought we might continue our tradition of traveling over the Christmas holidays," my mother added.

I nodded. Of course. I hadn't expected any different. "Where are you going this year?"

"Well," my dad said slowly, "we were hoping to perhaps go out there."

"Out here? Aloha Lagoon?" I gaped at the photo of my mother on my phone screen. They'd want to see *me*?

"Yes, of course, dear," my mother said. "If it's okay with you. We understand you would be…working." She said working the same way some people discuss an infant's dirty diaper.

"No, of course not," I said then realized that was the wrong way to say it. "I mean yes, of course you're welcome to come. I'd love it!"

"Excellent," my mother said. "Now, for Thanksgiving, why don't you send the dates you would like to be here, and we will get tickets for you both."

Both?

"For me…" I started to say then faltered. "And?"

"Dex, of course," said my mother. My father was conspicuously silent. "If the boy would like to come. I imagine it will be quite cold for him, but there's so much for you to show him here."

For the first time, possibly ever, I wondered if I was more like my mother than I realized.

"I can ask him. I think it would be fun," I said. "I might need a day or two to get an answer from him, if that's okay."

I swear my father sighed in relief in the background.

"Oh?" my mother asked. "He's not there with you?"

"No," I said. "He's in the hospital." I facepalmed then rushed on, "It's six a.m. on a Sunday. Of course he's not here. My new cat is though."

"Hospital?" my father said.

"Cat?" my mother said.

"Yes, the animals in the shelter escaped, and we went and helped regather them, but the cat followed me home. He's very pretty. I think you'll like him. I've named him Doyle."

"Doyle?" my mother repeated uncertainly.

"Why is Dex in the hospital, Kiki?" my father asked.

"He was in a little car accident. He's fine, but they kept him overnight in case he has a concussion," I said, squeezing my eyes shut and willing them to ask more about the cat than the accident.

There was a drawn-out silence, and then my mother spoke up.

"I hope he is fine, Katherine," she said. "I'm glad it was minor."

"Yes," my father agreed. "Please give him our best. And send the dates when you get a chance, please."

"And a picture of your new kitty," added my mother.

Who was this woman?

* * *

I recounted the uncharacteristic phone call to Auntie Akamai as we drove toward the Harris's pineapple plantation. Auntie Akamai was quite pleased with the news. She had been playing peacemaker between my parents and me ever since I arrived in Aloha Lagoon. I considered for a moment inviting her to New York too, but it would negate the romantic aspect of fall in New York City with Dex.

"What are you going to do about the Hallo-wedding?" Auntie Akamai asked. "I'm pretty sure Dex won't be able to go now."

Ugh. "Gosh, I hadn't even thought about it yet," I said, pulling a shank of hair forward to play with.

"Both hands on the wheel, please," Auntie Akamai said.

"Sorry." I returned my errant hand to the wheel and focused on the road.

"What were your costumes?" Auntie Akamai asked.

"Dex had suggested Fred and Daphne from *Scooby-Doo,"* I said, "but that included a giant brown dog."

"What?" Auntie Akamai laughed. "A dog?"

"Yes. He wants to adopt a dog," I said. "Not just a dog—an enormous dog! A Great Dane!"

"Wow. I wonder what Doyle will think," Auntie Akamai said.

"Yeah, I don't know." I laughed. "I'm wondering what his mom will think!"

Auntie Akamai shook her head. "Probably not excited about it. But what are you going to do about a costume now?"

I shrugged. "I hadn't gotten anything for it yet, so I have no idea. It needs to be easy though, at this point."

"How about Nancy Drew?" Auntie Akamai asked. "It would be easy, especially since there are so many versions. You do have a plaid skirt though, right?"

"That's a great idea!" I said. "I do have a plaid skirt and a matching sweater. And I wouldn't have to do anything too weird with my hair. But how will people know I'm Nancy Drew?"

Auntie Akamai waved a hand to dismiss my concern. "I have a magnifying glass. That should help."

I nodded. "Yes! And maybe a flashlight?"

Auntie Akamai nodded her approval. "Yes. And take the next right, right after the roadside stand."

Of course, it was a shaved ice stand which featured pineapples. I slowed to turn into a long drive, up to a fancy estate house. I parked the car at the end of the parking lot, as I wasn't confident parking between cars yet. As we got out, a stressed-looking man with a clipboard approached us.

"We are about to leave. Please make haste to the train," he said, pointing toward the estate house. Then he stopped abruptly, looked from us to his list and back to us and our confused faces. "Oh. Um. Are you the Smiths?" he asked.

We both shook our heads.

"Oh, sorry. Our last reservations haven't arrived." He glanced at his watch then looked at us hopefully. "Did you want to take the train tour of the plantation?"

"No, we're here to see someone," Auntie Akamai said. "But thank you, son. You're doing a great job."

The man beamed at her. "Mahalo!" Then he turned and ran for the "train," which was more accurately described as a golf cart pulling a half dozen extra seating cars.

We headed for the front doors of the estate, which was a long, two-story building with a porch that ran the entire length in the front. We climbed the stairs, and I held the door open for Auntie Akamai then followed her to a long reception desk dominating the entryway.

"Aloha," she said to the young woman behind the counter. "I wanted to talk to Nathan Harris. I'm a family friend."

But before the woman could pick up the phone, a voice came from above her.

"Auntie, come on up," said Nathan Junior from a balcony running the length of the room. "I've been expecting you."

CHAPTER TWENTY-FIVE

We settled into couches in a sitting area at one side of Nathan Junior's office. He offered us water from a pitcher on the coffee table, but we declined. We all sat for a moment, everyone staring awkwardly at one another. Finally, Nathan spoke.

"I didn't try to kill my mother," he said. "As you can imagine, I don't see any point."

I just watched him. I had never met him before now, so I didn't have a previous image to compare to, but he did look thin in body and in hair.

Auntie Akamai assured him we didn't think he was trying to kill his mother. "How is she doing this morning?"

"Fine," Nathan said. "She's a tough woman. Just a bump on the head really."

Auntie Akamai smiled. "Wonderful. I've been so worried."

"So why are you here?" Nathan asked. "You could've called to find this out."

Truth was, we already had called the hospital and were already aware of her condition.

Auntie Akamai clasped her hands on her lap. "We were wondering more about other people who will, or might, inherit from her."

Nathan sighed and looked at his hands. "I've already spoken to the detective about my brother and *that* woman," he said. "As far as I'm concerned, I have no dog in this fight."

"I take it you don't like your sister-in-law," I said.

He leveled his gaze on me. "Not much to like, to be honest. Jennifer's quite a piece of work."

Auntie Akamai tutted at him. "Now, Nathan, she's been good for your brother and for Noah."

Nathan gave a short laugh and followed it with a cough. "Yeah, sure."

Auntie Akamai frowned at him.

"You don't find it interesting that Cain's first wife died after he met Jennifer?" he asked. "Sure, not fishy at all."

"Wait," I said. "How'd she die?" I had assumed it was after an illness.

Auntie Akamai pursed her lips. "I don't think it's related, Nathan."

He shook his head and barked a laugh out. "Don't be such a Pollyanna, Auntie."

She raised a single eyebrow, and he immediately apologized.

"I'm sorry. I find it laughable no one is considering how Marti died," he said.

Wait. *Marti?* Where had I heard her name before? Had I heard it before? I looked at Auntie Akamai.

"Who is Marti?" I asked.

"Cain's first wife—Noah's birth mother," Auntie Akamai told me. Then she turned back to Nathan. "I'm sure they checked after her death. Don't accuse people about natural occurrences."

"Natural?" Nathan laughed again. "Like my impending death? How natural is this?"

Auntie Akamai frowned and looked at the ground.

Nathan looked at me. "I have cancer eating away my lungs." His stare was disconcerting. "I've never smoked a cigarette in my life."

I gazed back at him. "I'm really sorry to hear that, Mr. Harris. But honestly, none of this is what we came to ask you about."

He narrowed his eyes slightly. "Then what?"

I resisted the urge to shift uncomfortably in my chair. "We were wondering if you have any children."

Nathan frowned. "No, I don't have any children. I've never had much time to date, let alone have a relationship long enough to create a child."

I opened my mouth to remind him one does not need but a few minutes to create a child, when he raised a finger.

"No accidental children either," he reiterated. "But what does that have to do with anything?"

"I was wondering if Noah is the only heir," I said.

"Unfortunately," Nathan said. "At least *unfortunately* in my mother's eyes. Oliana is not a fan of Noah."

"Why?" I asked.

"His mother," Nathan said simply. "Marti stole her favorite son—Cain—away from her. Typical Mommy Dearest type stuff."

Auntie Akamai sat forward. "Wait a moment. Who were you accusing of killing Marti? Your mother or Jennifer?"

Nathan shrugged. "Both? Either? I don't know." He shook his head. "Cain and Jennifer met by the hand of my mother. Oliana used to like her." He laughed and started coughing again. He reached for his water and drank with a shaking hand then returned the glass to the table. "They don't like each other now, but it doesn't mean they didn't once."

Auntie Akamai shot me a look, and I raised a shoulder a teeny bit. She looked back at Nathan. "Thank you for your time, Nathan."

He nodded but didn't stand when we did and didn't walk us to the door.

* * *

"He's changed a lot over the years," Auntie Akamai said once we were back in the car. "The older he got, the more angry he seemed to get at his parents. Most kids grow out of that, but he never did. And now he's probably additionally angry about being sick."

"Why was he angry? Because he didn't want to follow in the business?" I asked. I knew better than most that pressure, but I also knew how to navigate it successfully. I could imagine, though, how jaded I would be, and how angry at myself and the world I would have been, had I simply bent to my parents' wishes.

She nodded. "He never stood up to them. And I imagine it would have been very hard to. Nash, Oliana's husband, had a very strong personality."

Well, that's quite the euphemism.

Auntie Akamai looked at her watch. "Let's go see how Dex is doing. Shall we grab some flowers?" she asked, and when I agreed, she gave me directions to a store on the way. As I was about to pull out of the plantation driveway, she pointed to the roadside store.

"Let's grab him some fresh pineapple. He loves the stuff."

We ended up getting shaved ice with fresh pineapple and coconut shavings on top as well as a container of the same for Dex. We sat at a table with an umbrella to eat our shaved ice, as it was a gorgeous day, though maybe not hot enough for the frozen treat. It got me shivering by the time I was halfway through, so after, I hurried to the warm car.

As we drove to the Kekoas' house to see Dex, we discussed Nathan.

I looked over at Auntie Akamai. "So do you think there's anything to Nathan's accusation that Cain's first wife was murdered?"

She shook her head. "I doubt it. I'm not even sure why he would say something like that!"

"What was her name again?" I asked.

"Marti," said Auntie Akamai before sticking a spoonful of pineapple and coconut in her mouth.

"Why does that sound familiar to me?" I asked. "Is there someone else here with that name, or is it someone from college or something?"

Auntie Akamai gasped and grabbed her forehead. "Brain freeze!"

I giggled—I had never in my life had the sensation.

It only took a few minutes to get to the Kekoas' house. After a quick knock on the door, Auntie Akamai let herself in. "Kahiau? Sarah?" she called out softly. We were surprised when Dex's head popped over the back of the couch.

"I'm here. Dad went to the shop and Mom to the store," he said, and then his eyes fell onto the plastic dome of shaved ice in Auntie Akamai's hand. He grinned. "For me?"

"Of course, *keiki*," Auntie Akamai cooed as she went around to the front of the couch and sat on the couch near his feet. I stayed by the door, tears suddenly springing to my eyes.

Dex was covered with a blanket, and *It's the Great Pumpkin, Charlie Brown* was on the TV but the volume down low. An ice pack sat on the coffee table in front of him.

"I should get injured more often," Dex joked. Then he caught sight of me standing frozen by the door. "Kiki?"

I rushed over, and kneeling on the floor next to him, I went to throw my arms around his neck but was stopped at the sight of the sling holding his arm and collarbone stationary. Instead, I leaned forward and gave him a peck on the cheek and another near his stitches on the side of his head. That side of his head was shaved, giving him an 80s punk-style haircut which was going to have to be fixed. Soon.

Dex put his good hand to my cheek and wiped away an errant tear. "I'm okay, Kiki. I'm okay," he said soothingly.

I sat back, wiping my eyes. I kept ahold of his hand.

"Tell us what happened, *keiki*," Auntie Akamai said.

"Well, everything was fine until the first stop sign. I tried to stop, but when I pushed the brake, nothing happened," he said. His eyes darted between his frozen treat and us a few times before I got the hint and dropped his hand. He took a moment to shovel in some ice and fruit, humming his appreciation.

"We saw you went through the sign," I said, finally trusting my voice to speak without crying.

"I was gonna tan your hide for driving like that with Oliana in the car!" Auntie Akamai said, shaking her head. "Kiki said you usually stop at the signs, so we should have known something was wrong then." She raised a hand to her eyes and sighed.

"Thank goodness no one else was in that intersection," I added.

Dex nodded. "And we kept going. I didn't accelerate, but the car continued to speed up. I kept pumping the brakes, but nothing. There was a dashboard light warning of a problem, and Oliana noticed and asked me what was wrong," he said. "I didn't want to scare her, but she was amazing. Cool as a cucumber. Once I told her the brakes weren't working, she called 9-1-1 and told them."

Auntie Akamai nodded. "They did arrive quickly, all things considered."

"Once we were on the highway, it was okay to be going the speed we were, but the car wasn't slowing down at all," Dex said, shivering from either the memory or the cold treat. "Oliana and I decided pulling the emergency brake slowly would be a good plan. It didn't work out like we thought it would." He leaned back and set the shaved ice container on his lap.

"It's amazing you both weren't hurt more than you were," Auntie Akamai whispered, and I could see the emotion getting to her too. "I don't know what I would have done…"

"But we're fine, Auntie," Dex said, taking her hand. "Everything is okay."

"Except the fact that someone did it intentionally," I said.

"Well, yeah, except for that," Dex said. "I don't think the police know anything yet. Do you guys?"

Auntie Akamai and I both shook our heads.

Dex looked at me. "You're still going to go to the Hallo-wedding, right?" he asked. "My mom says the doctor said no, but I think she made it up."

I rolled my eyes. "You have a broken arm and a broken collarbone, new stitches in your head, and a most hideous haircut."

Dex frowned. "I rather like it. I'd be a great zombie, staggering around like this."

I felt my eyes go wide.

"I'm kidding, Kiki," Dex said. "I guess I'm going to be getting a haircut soon." He faked crying for a moment, and we all laughed.

"That's okay, right?" I asked. "If I still go?"

"Of course," Dex said with a smile and took my hand. "With Cain and Jennifer Harris catering, there's another opportunity to get eyes on them."

Auntie Akamai grunted. "I hadn't thought of that, but it's true. Maybe I should go too," she said then laughed.

"Oh, you should!" I said. "If I go as Nancy Drew, you should come as Miss Marple!"

Auntie Akamai laughed. "A younger and well-fed Miss Marple." She pointed at Dex's treat container. "Do you want me to put this in the freezer? You look a bit peaked."

"Yeah, I guess. I do feel a little tired." Dex gestured at the TV. "And the best part is coming on."

We laughed and took the barely veiled hint. I gave Dex a kiss, and Auntie Akamai gave him one as well after handing his ice pack back to him. "Put this on wherever is hurting," she called over her shoulder as we left.

"I'm not feeling any pain," he assured us. "No pain at all!"

"I could fix that," I muttered, and Auntie Akamai swatted my arm.

CHAPTER TWENTY-SIX

Our next stop was to talk to Margaux. We found the former bartender in her yard, picking up plant detritus, presumably a result of the rain.

Auntie Akamai opened the gate, and I followed her into Margaux's yard. Margaux dropped a handful of twigs and leaves into a paper yard waste bag and wiped her gloved hands together.

"Hi, ladies. What can I do for you?" Margaux asked with a smile. "Would you like some tea?"

"Sure, in a second," Auntie Akamai said. "First, I'd like to see the cutting from Celine's Bougainvillea."

Margaux tipped her head and stared at her friend. "All right," she said slowly. "Follow me."

A nervous trill went up my spine, but I shook it off as I followed them.

As she led us along the path, Margaux removed her gloves and slapped them against her thigh. When we got to the small greenhouse in the back, she tucked her gloves under one arm and dug a key out of the pocket of her loose khaki pants. After unlocking the door, she pushed it open and stood aside.

Auntie Akamai walked in, but I gestured to Margaux to go ahead in before me. She rolled her eyes but followed Auntie Akamai.

We stood around a rustic rectangular worktable littered with planting soil and discarded plastic pots. I glanced up at Margaux to see her watching Auntie Akamai closely and realized with a start that there were several sharp-looking tools hanging behind her, within reach.

Margaux glanced at me. "Were you born in a barn, Kiki? Close the door behind you!"

I was taken aback by her tone but did as she said.

Margaux turned to Auntie Akamai. "Okay, yes, you see I have a cutting from Celine's plant. But I didn't kill her to get it." She slapped her gardening gloves down on the table. "Do you really think that of me? I mean, if you do, I guess we are not as good of friends as I thought."

Auntie Akamai raised her hands in surrender. "I don't think you killed Celine. And I don't think you did it to get a cutting of her Bougainvillea. I wanted to see if Kiki was right about the cutting being from Celine's plant." Auntie Akamai nodded at me.

Margaux relaxed slightly. "Okay, then." She reached out a finger and touched a blossom. "Her sister, Bette, brought me a cutting. We don't know what will happen to her original, what will happen to the house. I just wanted to have something to remember Celine by." Tears filled her eyes and spilled out.

Auntie Akamai opened her arms to her, and the two women embraced.

I fidgeted, using a finger to sweep errant potting soil into a little hill then turned and looked out the side window.

On the windowsill was a book. I leaned over to read the title. *Natural Healing Through Botany.*

The sounds of sniffling lessened, and then I heard nose-blowing. I picked up the book and turned around, flipping through it as I did.

Margaux zeroed in on the book in my hand. "Lemme guess. Now you have a question about that."

Auntie Akamai peered over, so I held the book out to her. She took it and flipped it open to a random page.

"What was in the bottle you gave the sous chef at the World Fusion Café?" I asked.

Margaux's eyes widened. Then she sighed and shook her head. She then took the book back and flipped the pages back and forth until she found a particular one. "You guys are pretty good," she said. She laid the book on the table and pointed at it.

I leaned over to read the page about plants that would help…

"Acne," I read. I looked up at Margaux. "The sous chef has acne?"

Margaux held up her hands and smiled. "Not as bad as she used to have." She then looked at Auntie Akamai. "I'd never poison anyone, let alone Celine."

Auntie Akamai nodded. "Not Oliana either, right?"

Margaux frowned. "Of course not. Not you either." She paused and tipped her head. "Why do you ask about Oliana?"

Auntie Akamai and I exchanged a look.

"Have you not heard about the car accident yet?" Auntie Akamai asked her.

"What?" Margaux asked. "Who was in an accident?"

"Dex and Oliana—he was driving her home," I said.

"Oh, that's awful!" Margaux's hand flew to her throat. "Are they okay?"

Auntie Akamai looked me in the eye then turned back to Margaux. "Dex has several broken bones and stitches. Oliana is bad enough that she hasn't been released and I can't get in to see her."

It wasn't a lie, *technically*. Just laid on a bit *thick*.

"What happened?" Margaux asked, her hand on her throat trembling.

"Someone cut her brakes," Auntie Akamai said gravely. "Someone tried to kill Oliana, having no idea Dex would be there as well."

My eyes had a mind of their own as they went to the wall of garden sheers behind Margaux.

Auntie Akamai followed my eyes, and Margaux did as well. Both turned toward the wall.

Margaux turned back around, her eyes rolling. "You clearly don't know much about cars, do you, Kiki?" She looked at Auntie Akamai pleadingly. "I would never hurt any of you, Akamai!"

And again with the hugging and the crying.

* * *

"Well, that was therapeutic if nothing else." Auntie Akamai took a deep breath once we were back in the car. She held it a moment then slowly let it out, which I recognized as being from the yoga classes I got her interested in watching.

"I don't think we were suspecting her. We just had loose ends," I pointed out. "We have a better idea about the bottle she gave the sous chef now."

"If she was being straight with us," Auntie Akamai said.

My head whipped to her. "What? You think she may not be?"

Auntie Akamai raised a shoulder. "As much as we liked and included her, she probably always felt like an outsider, to an extent. Plus, she used to do some acting in theater."

"Hmm." I stopped at a stop sign. "Where are we going now, by the way?"

Auntie Akamai pointed left. "We need to go let the shelter know about Doyle. Might as well drop by. It's so close."

I nodded. Part of me was a little afraid they would say I had to take him back. I could almost see the hurt on his little furry face.

I parked in the lot, and we walked into the NASH Animal Shelter. The same volunteer, Linda, was working the desk.

We stopped in front of her, and I waited until Auntie Akamai prodded me with her elbow.

"Oh, okay," I said, propping my elbows on the counter. "Hi. So…we have one of the cats that got loose the other day. I would like to keep him but figured we should let you know."

"Oh, okay. Is it the one we called Loki, by any chance?" Linda asked.

"Yes!" I smiled. "Or at least I think so. Gray?"

Linda nodded. "We usually chip and neuter before adoption. Do you think you could bring him back so we could do that?"

Auntie Akamai nodded her approval. "Of course."

I agreed. "When should I bring him back?"

Linda flipped through her calendar while I pulled up my own on my phone. "Tuesday?" she suggested. "By eight in the morning?"

I tapped it into my phone. "Sure thing."

Auntie Akamai watched our exchange, but when it was over, she turned to me. "Let's pop in and look at the dogs." She looked at Linda. "My nephew is apparently interested in a Great Dane here?"

Linda smiled. "Of course! Scooby. He's a Great Dane mix." She pointed down the hall to the right as the phone on the desk rang. "Do you mind looking yourself?" she asked, looking pointedly at the telephone.

"No problem," Auntie Akamai said and linked her arm into mine before leading me down the hall.

I'll admit I was curious to see the dog as well, but not so much interested. Dogs were never my thing. But once we entered the long kennel room, I saw Auntie Akamai's motivation.

Noah.

CHAPTER TWENTY-SEVEN

Auntie Akamai went immediately to the chain link gate of the nearest run, acting like she hadn't noticed Noah standing farther inside the room.

Three or four runs down was the tall dog named Scooby. Auntie Akamai leaned over to peer in at him, though she didn't have to bend far to be eye to eye.

I read the information card. "He's part Great Dane and part boxer," I relayed to Auntie Akamai. "Two years old, so"—I looked the dog up and down—"maybe full grown?"

"Yes," said Noah from behind us. "He's probably as big as he's going to get." He moved next to me and pointed at the dog's front paws. "You can get an idea by their paws, if they have grown into them or not."

While the dog's paws were big, they were to scale for the rest of his frame.

"Are you interested in this dog?" he asked.

Auntie Akamai and I both shook our heads.

"My boyfriend Dex wants him," I said, in order to explain our interest.

Noah nodded. "Yeah, I saw him here."

"You must really love animals," Auntie Akamai said. "Do you want to be a vet?"

He grinned. "I'd love to be. But coming here is a way to spend time with my grandma."

Auntie Akamai nodded. "Of course."

I stared at her. I knew Oliana donated money to the shelter—enough so it was named after the family—but I had a hard time envisioning her volunteering here.

"I doubt I'll be able to be a vet though," Noah said, grinding the toe of his shoe into the cement. "My family has other ideas, you know?"

"I understand," I said. "My father owns a company he expected me to work at."

He tipped his head, confused. "Here?"

"No, in New York," I said, turning back to the dog. "How long does Dex have to make up his mind about Scooby?"

"He was pretty certain yesterday," he said.

I nodded. "Yeah, but he was in a car accident, remember? I'm not sure when he'll be able to take care of a dog, since he's got a broken arm."

Noah stuck his fingers through the chain link to scratch the dog's head. "What do you mean, remember? I didn't know."

I turned to Auntie Akamai and saw her eyebrows were in her hairline.

She leaned forward so she could see him directly. "He was driving the car your grandma was in. They were in the accident together."

Noah froze. "Grandma was in an accident?"

"Your Grandma Oliana," Auntie Akamai clarified.

"Oh," said Noah, his shoulders slumping back into normal teenager posture. "That grandmother. Yeah, I didn't know he was there. Is he okay?"

"Yeah, he'll be okay. Just not going to be able to handle this big guy," Auntie Akamai said, patting the chain link in front of us. She turned back to Noah. "Noah, you don't think anyone would want to hurt your Grandma Oliana on purpose, do you?"

He stared at the toe of his shoe as he continued to grind it into the floor. "No."

I took a half step back and put a hand on his shoulder. "Noah, Miss Celine died by accident. Someone had been trying to poison Oliana."

Noah's head snapped up, and he stared at me. His face went from incredulous to angry to teetering on the edge of crying. He gave an adamant shake of his head and turned and ran down the length of the room before disappearing through a "no admittance—staff only" door.

Auntie Akamai and I exchanged a look.

She blew out a breath and crossed her arms. "That went well."

* * *

After we got home, my phone buzzed with a text from Analise, Celine's niece.

Heard about Dex. Is he ok?

Yeah, I texted back. *Broken bones and stitches in his head, but fine overall.*

That's good, I guess! Are you still going to the wedding?

I told her I was and was looking forward to hanging out with her. She sent back a thumbs-up emoji and said she was looking forward to it too.

My mom asked if I was taking a gift, she texted again. *Are you?*

I sent the scream-face emoji back. *OMG, I totally forgot about that.*

Let's go in on something together, she replied. *Like a gift card or something easy.*

We texted for a few more minutes, making our plan. Then I headed out for the store to get a card and a gift card. Since Auntie Akamai was taking a nap, I walked. I hadn't had to walk much anymore and found myself enjoying it. It was a beautiful day, and it cleared my mind and gave me time to think about the conversations from this morning.

I wasn't sure why I had been so surprised when Noah mentioned another grandmother. Of course he would have another. Or actually, probably two more, since he had a stepmother.

So who was his other grandmother? Auntie Akamai said "of course" about his grandmother working there, so she knew who he was talking about. Was it the other grandmother or Oliana?

And why was Margaux acting weird? I know the women were all friends, but she seemed to be grieving Celine more intensely than the other two, especially not having known her as long.

And what was the deal with Cain and Jennifer? Why were they so nice to my face then throwing me under the bus when anyone was around to listen?

Who knew Oliana's car would be at Auntie Akamai's house? It would have been visible from the road, so was it a crime of opportunity—not unlike Celine's poisoning? Who might have the expertise—or did one not need expertise anymore, with the internet at everyone's fingertips?

And last but not least, was Celine's poisoning intentional, like the cutting of Oliana's brake line had to have been?

Was someone out to get Auntie Akamai's mahjong friends?

Was Auntie Akamai next?

* * *

By the time I had gotten that last thought, I was practically running. I wanted to get to the store, get what I needed for the Hallo-wedding, and get home quickly to make sure Auntie Akamai was all right.

When I got to the store though, I calmed myself enough to do a little shopping for the Hallo-wedding costume too. I got a Nancy Drew-esque headband and ran through the rest of my outfit in my mind. Plaid skirt, sweater to wear over a button-up shirt, and Mary Janes. (Granted, they were platform Louboutin Mary Janes, but still…Mary Janes.) I grabbed a pair of tights that would make my mother faint ("*Tights* from a *grocery* store?") and a card then poured over the gift cards. Analise and I had decided on something useful and general, since we didn't know the couple well, so I ended up getting a generic credit card gift card.

I was running a little low on energy when I was done, so I stopped at the café for a pumpkin muffin and a skinny latte. While I was waiting at the counter, I heard a familiar voice behind me. Actually, two familiar voices. I slid behind a human shield beside me then peered around the rotund tourist. He grinned down at me. I smiled back but took a small step away, keeping him between the familiar voices and myself.

It was Stella and Jennifer.

What were they doing together? How did they even know each other? I strained to hear what they were saying.

The barista held up a cup and turned it to read my name, so I reached forward before he said it out loud.

"Thanks," I whispered, shooting him a smile. I slipped around the edge of the counter where an etched glass partition would hide me from the two women as they waited for their drinks. To further hide, I turned toward the back of the kitchen area, so if either woman were to glance over, they would only see my back.

Unfortunately, between the hissing of the espresso machines and the glass partition, I couldn't hear anything but a murmur, despite the conversation looking heated.

I helplessly watched them leave. I didn't learn anything other than the fact that they knew each other, which in itself didn't mean a darn thing.

CHAPTER TWENTY-EIGHT

When I returned back to the house, I was surprised to find Detective Ray sitting on the couch, staring down Doyle. The detective didn't appear to have much say in it, since the cat was sitting on his lap, glaring into his face.

"I don't think your cat likes me," he said, glancing up at me. "He should though. I've got cats on my shirt!"

Sure enough, there were tiny cats in arched, hissing positions scattered amongst the more typical flowers and trees of his Hawaiian-print shirt.

"Your shirts are great, Detective Ray," I said. "I love them."

Detective Ray grinned. "Thank you. You must have the same sense of humor as my wife. I don't know where she finds them, but she gets me a new one every year. I've got a good collection going."

"They're awesome," I told him then glanced at my phone. I had a new message from Shannon.

Did you figure out a costume for the wedding? the bride asked.

Yes, I typed back. *Nancy Drew.*

Oh... Zombie Nancy Drew? There was a pause, and then she sent the laughing emoji.

Um...sure, I said.

Didn't I mention everyone is supposed to be zombies?

I smacked a hand to my forehead.

Detective Ray broke eye contact with Doyle. "Everything okay?"

I flopped onto a chair just as Auntie Akamai came in with a tray of tea and finger cookies. "Yes, sort of. The Hallo-wedding bride told me I'm supposed to be a zombie of some sort. She asked if my Nancy Drew was going to be a zombie Nancy Drew." I sighed but smiled. "That will be fun though."

I texted Shannon back a thumbs-up and put my phone down.

"Kiki," said Auntie Akamai. "I woke up and you were gone. I'm sorry. I didn't know you needed to go somewhere."

"It's okay," I said, waving off her worry. "I still know how to walk." I held up the bag of purchases. "Analise and I went in on a wedding gift."

"Oh, I'm sure they're not expecting one from total strangers!" Auntie Akamai frowned.

I shrugged. "It's what we do, right?" I set the bag down and shook my head at it. "Looks like I need to go back and get zombie makeup."

"Oh, Stella next door should have something you can use. She used to do face painting at fairs and such. She can get you set right up." Auntie Akamai nodded like it was a done deal. She turned her attention to Detective Ray. "So you haven't said what brings you by, Ray."

Doyle stalked off his lap and over to mine, where he curled up sweetly and went to sleep.

Detective Ray shook his head at the cat and reached forward for his mug and a cookie. "I wanted to give you an update on the accident."

Auntie Akamai sat and made herself comfortable. "The brakes?"

He nodded. "They were definitely disconnected, but there were no prints left behind."

"Cut?" I asked, thinking of Margaux's wall of plant shears.

"Yes," Detective Ray said.

"How do you do that?" Auntie Akamai asked. "Are scissors strong enough?"

Detective Ray shook his head. "Brake lines are metal, so it would take something stronger."

"Plant cutters?" I asked.

Detective Ray frowned. "I don't think so. I'd have to ask the techs. Why?"

"Just curious how easy it is to do," I said.

He shook his head. "No clue. I don't even know where the brakes lines are in my car, but I suppose it wouldn't be too hard to look it up."

"The joy of the internet." I stroked Doyle as he lay curled like a croissant on my lap.

Detective Ray nodded. "Exactly. So the bigger question is who had access to her car." He turned to Auntie Akamai. "You don't have a doorbell camera, and there's nothing on your neighbor's. But do you have any other cameras?"

Auntie Akamai shook her head. "Never felt like I needed one."

Detective Ray's eyebrows rose. "Consider the past year…"

I glanced at Auntie Akamai. "I can pay for it."

Auntie Akamai waved a hand. "Paying for it isn't the issue. Needing it is the question. Do I really want to feel so paranoid that I need a camera on my front door?"

"It doesn't make you paranoid," I told her. "A lot of people have them now to watch for packages or even to know if they want to answer the door or not."

Auntie Akamai shook her head. "That's not our way. Doors are not meant to be closed and unwelcoming."

Detective Ray and I shared a glance. He leaned forward and put his elbows on his knees. "I understand all that, Akamai. Of course I do. But I am telling you, as a policeman and as a friend, perhaps it's time to get one."

* * *

Later, over a simple dinner of sandwiches, Auntie Akamai and I discussed the idea of a doorbell camera again.

"I worry the neighbors won't like it. It is their privacy as well," she said.

I held up a finger. "Could be for their safety too, don't forget."

Auntie Akamai studied her sandwich for a moment, like it held the answers. "Isn't it accepting things could happen?"

"What makes it any different than the security light?" I asked. I took a big bite and chewed as I waited for her to consider.

After a good amount of thinking, she nodded. "Okay. You're right."

"Detective Ray said one of your neighbors has a doorbell camera. Maybe you can ask them how to go about installing it," I said. "Who has it, do you know? I've never noticed one."

Auntie Akamai rolled her eyes. "Which would you expect? Stella Keawe." She shook her head. "Woman has to know everything going on."

I set down my sandwich. "Speaking of Stella…"

Auntie Akamai's eyebrows shot up. "Yes?"

"I saw her and Jennifer Harris getting coffee together when I was out," I said. "Is that weird at all?"

"Why would it be weird?" she asked.

"I mean, I know everyone knows everyone, but how do they know each other?" I asked. "It didn't look like they were having a particularly nice conversation."

Auntie Akamai snorted. "When have you ever had a nice conversation with either of them?"

I tipped my head back and forth. "True."

"That reminds me," Auntie Akamai said. "I need to see if she can do your makeup tomorrow."

"And yours," I reminded her. "I don't want to go without you."

Auntie Akamai gave me a funny look and reached for her phone. "What time do we need to be there?" she asked.

"Eight," I said.

Auntie Akamai's eyebrows shot up. "Eight a.m.? What if you have a dive?"

I shook my head. "Eight p.m.," I said. "It needs to be dark and creepy."

Auntie Akamai frowned but nodded her head. "Oh, of course." She texted with Stella while I went to check Doyle's food, water, and cat box. Doyle stalked after me and made a funny *brrrrrowww* sound.

"What is it, Doyle?" I asked, stopping and looking down at him.

He stood up on his hind legs with his front paws on my leg and let out a pitiful meow.

Maybe he wants to be picked up?

I reached down and picked him up under his "armpits" and draped him in my arms. He nuzzled my chin and started purring. "Aww, you just wanted some cuddles!"

I carried him with me back to the living room and sat on the couch. Auntie Akamai was now sitting in her chair, watching *Jeopardy* on mute, the phone held to her ear. She occasionally made an *mhm* or *ahh* but other than those noises, it was clearly a one-sided conversation.

After way too many minutes of this, she finally rolled her eyes to the ceiling and held up a hand. "Okay, Stella, I'm sorry, I need to run. I'll see you tomorrow afternoon!"

It was a few more minutes before she was successful in disconnecting.

"We need to find that woman a new hobby," she said.

CHAPTER TWENTY-NINE

The next morning, Kahiau and I took turns diving and manning the boat. As usual, with the early morning dives, we were back by lunchtime. In the heavier tourist season, we might have afternoon dives, too, but we'd kept the afternoon clear since it was Halloween.

Kahiau dropped me off at home, and I hurried inside. Auntie Akamai was in the kitchen, throwing together a salad for our lunch.

"I figured you'd probably want to eat light since there'll be a lot of food and candy the rest of the day," she said, setting the wooden bowl of greens and vegetables on the kitchen table.

"Sounds good to me!" I said, not mentioning the pound of candy I'd already eaten today.

We sat, and Auntie Akamai watched as I dished up my salad and drizzled her homemade citrus vinaigrette on it.

"I spoke with Detective Ray this morning," Auntie Akamai said casually as she served herself.

My mouth was full of lettuce, so I just raised my eyebrows and nodded my head to indicate I was listening.

"I told him I was a little concerned about Margaux's behavior, as well as Noah's." Auntie Akamai stared at her lunch as if wanting to climb into the bowl as well. "He said to continue to keep our eyes and ears open. And he said something odd about Margaux…"

I sped up my chewing rate and swallowed. "What?"

Auntie Akamai hesitated a moment. "Well, he couldn't find much about her before she came here."

"I don't understand," I said. "What, like they did a background check and couldn't find out anything about her?"

Auntie Akamai nodded. "Exactly. At least, not much."

We both took bites of food and pondered in silence while we chewed.

"What did they find?" I asked after I swallowed.

"When she arrived in Hawaii and that she flew in from Los Angeles," Auntie Akamai said and shrugged.

"She's hiding something. But why?"

Auntie Akamai shook her head. "I have no idea."

* * *

A few hours later, Stella knocked on the door.

"Are you ladies ready to be zombie-fied?" She grinned up at me after I opened the door. Her cheetah-print glasses were propped up on top of her head, which now had black streaks added to the purple ones. Her skin was an unhealthy gray hue, with dark circles around her eyes and a very disgusting, chunky wound on her cheek. She wore a painter's smock, covered in paint.

Auntie Akamai joined us and gave Stella a once-over. "You look great, but where's your makeup box?" she asked her.

"At my house, of course," Stella said. "It's too much to carry over here."

"Oh. I guess I misunderstood," Auntie Akamai said, frowning. She waved her hand to usher me ahead of her. "Let's go, then."

As we walked across the lawn to the next house, Stella turned and looked me up and down. "Are you a certain character or just a person?" she asked me.

"Well, I was going for Nancy Drew. I left my props behind though," I said. "Do you think I need to tear up my clothes or anything?"

Stella raised an eyebrow. "How expensive are they?"

I looked down at my outfit as I walked. I had a wool Burberry plaid skirt with beige sweater set with the cardigan buttoned. "Not very. Other than the shoes, but I don't have them on yet." I was wearing slip-on sandals with my tights. "I'd rather not damage the skirt though."

Stella then gave Auntie Akamai a once-over. "And you, Akamai? Who are you?"

Auntie Akamai looked down at her own outfit, one of her regular colorful muumuus. "I think I'm just me."

"A zombie you," I reminded her.

We followed Stella up the steps to her bungalow. I noted the doorbell camera as she opened her door for us to go in.

"Shall we do Kiki first?" Stella asked, rubbing her hands together with glee. She had two chairs set up next to a table covered in canisters and paintbrushes and led me to one of the chairs.

She started by making my exposed skin an undead gray, explaining it wouldn't transfer to the car seats and would stay on until I scrubbed it off with soap. After a base coat of deadness, she started on gruesome wounds.

Auntie Akamai hovered over us until Stella, with an eyeroll, sent her off to make tea. I was a little surprised to see she knew her way around Stella's kitchen with ease.

"Acting like she can do this better," Stella muttered as Auntie Akamai left the room.

I tried to look around, but Stella would forcibly move my face whichever way she wanted. I found myself wondering if she had any children other than the one daughter who'd passed away. She was a little rough.

"What did you do when you worked, Miss Stella?" I asked when she was creating blood dripping out of my right ear.

"Boring stuff in an office, but my passion work is art," she said, gesturing around. "All these paintings are mine."

I could only see one over her shoulder. It was a pretty good beachscape, and I was fairly certain it was from right out back of the house. "They're very nice," I said.

Stella snorted. "Well, that's nice of you to say, but I know you grew up with Rembrandts and Caravaggios."

I restrained myself from laughing out loud. "Not really."

Auntie Akamai walked back in carrying three mugs. "Your work is lovely, Stella." She set the mugs on the table, pushing two toward us. "Kiki, the painting of my bungalow, on the wall by the door? Stella painted that for me for Christmas one year."

"Ah," I said. "I've always wondered about it."

"I did the one of the NASH animal shelter for them, but Oliana won't let them hang it. It sits in a closet." Stella sniffed her indignation.

"Why?" I asked.

Instead of answering, Stella moved my head roughly the other way and started prattling on about someone who insisted on feeding the birds on the pier and another woman who had gotten her nails painted a scandalous color.

For an artist with purple hair and neon-pink reader glasses, it was an interesting thing to be horrified by.

In my line of sight now was a portrait of a young woman. I would never say it out loud, but Stella was better at painting landscapes than people. I studied the face while she worked on open wound above my left eye.

Finally, she finished and showed me the results of her work in the bathroom mirror.

"Ew, that's disgusting," I said, leaning closer to the mirror to inspect it. "It's perfect! You did a wonderful job."

Stella puffed up, said thank you, and led me back out to where Auntie Akamai was taking her seat for her turn. A photo in the hall caught my eye, and I stopped to stare at it.

Why did she have a photo of Noah on her wall?

After a moment, I continued on to the dining room. I made a circuit of the room, coming to a stop in front of the portrait of the young lady. I wanted to ask who it was, but my other questions had gone ignored, so I didn't bother.

Auntie Akamai obviously noticed where I paused and offered an answer despite me not asking.

"That's Stella's daughter, Marti," she said, interrupting Stella's stream of consciousness gossiping.

"Marti," I repeated. That must be why the name had sounded familiar when I heard it before. I struggled to think where I had heard it before now.

I continued my tour around the mostly open concept area, into her living room. On the top of a bookcase were several framed photos, so I headed over to look at them. There were several more of Marti at various ages and a few more of Noah. Then one caught my eye, and I picked it up to look closer. It appeared to be a family photo. In it was a little Noah, Stella's daughter Marti, and Cain Harris.

CHAPTER THIRTY

I picked up the framed photo to stare at it. I was certain the father in the family photo was Cain Harris, which made sense with Noah being in it as well. But filling the role of mother was Marti, Stella's daughter.

Marti's daughter, who had passed away.

Cain Harris's first wife passed away.

Which made Stella the other grandma.

I closed my eyes, mentally face-palming myself. (I didn't want to actually touch my face and risk messing up my oozing wounds.)

I shook my head and set the photo back down on the cabinet, realizing with horror I had transferred a fingerprint of undead gray onto the frame.

I lifted the edge of my cardigan and tried to wipe it off, but it stayed. *Dang it.* Not only had I ruined the frame, but she'd be able to tell I had been snooping. I thought she said this paint wouldn't transfer!

I glanced behind me, but the women couldn't see me from their positions at the table in the dining room. Maybe she wouldn't notice it and forget about the body paint?

And this didn't bode well for Auntie Akamai's car.

Why hadn't Auntie Akamai mentioned Noah and Stella were related? I mean, this was pretty important, especially if people were implying Marti had been murdered. And this was definitely the cause of the bad blood between Oliana and Stella. And explained how Stella and Jennifer knew each other.

I left the living room and returned to the dining room to find Stella standing over Auntie Akamai, holding a large pair of silver scissors like a dagger.

I gasped, and they both turned to me.

"What?" Stella said innocently.

Auntie Akamai understood my first impression. "She's making cuts in my clothing."

I let out my breath. "Oh, of course. We should do a few on mine."

"Yes, of course. Especially your tights." Stella looked pointedly at my legs. "We should gum up those gams with some wounds too."

I took a glance at my watch after she turned away. We still had some time.

I stood and watched as Stella made some artful cuts and put wounds inside a few of them. When Auntie Akamai looked at me, I tipped my head slightly and gave her a hard look. She tried to raise her eyebrows, but one of them was plastered in place, giving her an almost comical, lopsided look. I kept eye contact a good long time so she knew I was irritated about something.

Once Stella made some artful cuts in Auntie Akamai's dress and stained the cloth around them, she waved me forward. She pointed at the chair. "Why don't you stand on there?"

I stepped up onto one of her dining room chairs and faced her.

Stella very carefully made a tear in my grocery store tights and gooped it up with paint. When she was done, she straightened her back and glanced up at me. "Not the skirt, right?"

"Right," I said. I stepped down, careful not to wipe my leg wound paint off on her chair.

She made a few discolored areas and tears in my sweater then stood back to look me up and down. "What do you think, Akamai?"

Auntie Akamai stood back and surveyed me, mug in hand. "I think she looks hideous." She raised her drink as if toasting us. "Excellent job!"

Stella's gray hue turned pinkish as she grinned. "Thank you so much, Akamai."

"Thank *you* so much, Miss Stella," I said to her. "You did a wonderful job."

"You're welcome, Kiki." She beamed, clapped her hands. "Let's go!"

Auntie Akamai and I exchanged a look.

"I didn't realize you were going, Stella," said Auntie Akamai.

"Of course," Stella said, looking at Auntie Akamai like she had two zombie heads instead of one. "Why do you think I have makeup on too?" With that, she unbuttoned her painting smock to show us a semiformal skirt suit set in a shiny material that looked like it was from the midnineties. She had zombied it up, so clearly she knew it was out of date and trashable. "I'm helping the Harrises with the catering, but I'll take my portable kit in case someone needs to be killed off."

At *killed off*, she raised the huge shiny scissors and made a stabbing motion then cackled. She turned and tucked them into a bag, which she swung onto her shoulder.

"Shall I drive?" Stella asked.

"Um, sure," Auntie Akamai said, shooting me another look. "Kiki, do you need to go grab your props?"

I nodded. "And my shoes."

"I'll go with you and check on Paulie," she said and turned to follow me.

"I'll come too," said Stella.

"That's not necessary, Stella," said Auntie Akamai.

"I don't mind," Stella shot back and followed us to the door.

When we were back on the porch, I looked back to see her pause just inside the door and glance to the right.

Where the family photos were displayed.

I quickly turned to Auntie Akamai. "Auntie," I whispered.

Auntie Akamai turned back with raised eyebrows.

"No whispering!" Stella called out in a creepy singsong as she slammed her front door and joined us. She threw an arm around each one of us and hugged us to her. "Let's get going, girls!"

Her bag banged against my hip as we walked back to Auntie Akamai's house. *The bag with the giant scissors.*

Auntie Akamai called out to Paulie as we walked in the door, but once he saw who was with us, he immediately flew away to the kitchen. Auntie Akamai followed him, while I headed for my room to get my shoes and purse.

I opened my door and stopped abruptly to look for Doyle and was surprised when Stella bumped into me from behind. I spun around and looked at her.

She smiled up at me benignly.

I stared at her, but unable to think of something to say, I turned and continued on into my room.

And she followed.

I ignored her strange behavior and went to the closet to get my shoes. I sat on the end of the bed to put them on, and Doyle came out from under the bed and hopped up to rub against my elbow.

"Oh, you have this cat?" Stella said. "I didn't realize."

I nodded. "He followed me home somehow. I take him back tomorrow for the paperwork and medical stuff."

Stella then looked at my Louboutin shoes with their red soles. "Fancy," she said flatly.

I nodded. "I love my shoes, but there's rarely any reason or place to wear them here. This is land of the flip flops, which is fine by me!"

Stella stood and watched me put on my shoes like a demented zombie chaperone.

I didn't know what Auntie Akamai was doing in the kitchen with Paulie, but I figured I'd give her as much time as necessary. I fiddled with the straps on my shoes as long as possible, but not enough to be conspicuously time-wasting. Finally, I stood up and looked at Stella.

"Well, that took forever," she said.

"They're tiny straps. And I wanted to make sure the paint didn't transfer," I said.

Her eyebrows shot up. "Like it did to my picture frame?"

My stomach dropped.

Stella leaned toward me until her face was within inches of mine. "You shouldn't snoop, Nancy Drew."

Auntie Akamai spoke loudly from the doorway. "Here's the magnifying glass, Kiki."

I looked around Stella to see Auntie Akamai standing with fists on her hips. She was glaring at Stella.

I went to the bedside table and got my flashlight out of the drawer. It was a small, keychain type that I got as a freebie from a booth in college, a backup in case my phone was dead.

"Oh, Kiki, I thought this one would be more…theatrical," said Auntie Akamai, hefting up a flashlight about a foot and a half long and almost as thick as my forearm.

"Oh, that's great!" I picked up the envelope with the wedding card and gift and grabbed a bigger, cross-body-strap messenger-type bag from the closet. I put everything in it then gave Doyle a rub between his ears. Stella followed me closely out of the room, and Auntie Akamai closed the door behind her.

Stella turned back and looked at the door. "You lock the cat in there?" she asked.

"We haven't introduced Doyle and Paulie yet," I explained. "We're giving them a few days to adjust before trying."

Stella muttered something and shook her head as she led us to the front door.

We followed her out and back across the yards to her car. I slid into the back seat, while Auntie Akamai got into the front seat.

Stella settled herself in the driver's seat and started the car. Before putting it in gear, she turned around and gave me a scary smile. "Be sure you're buckled in."

CHAPTER THIRTY-ONE

In the back seat, I texted Auntie Akamai in the front and hoped she had her phone muted. Actually, I just hoped she had it with her. She'd been known to leave it at home sometimes. I was banking on now not being one of those times.

You never mentioned Stella is Noah's grandma!

I heard a faint buzz, and in front of me, Auntie Akamai's head bent down.

I'm sure I did, she replied.

No! I wrote and added an angry face emoji. (Not the really angry one, just the little bit angry one.)

Ok, she said back. *And?*

"It's not very polite to text instead of talking to the driver, Akamai," Stella said.

"I'm sorry," Auntie Akamai smoothly fibbed. "It's my son over on the Big Island, asking about my plans for the night. I don't hear from him every day."

I considered texting back. Her son probably would, right? And if I stopped, Stella would figure out Auntie Akamai and I were texting each other. I decided to go ahead and keep pretending to be her son.

This is clearly the source of bad blood between Oliana and Stella. And she's acting suspicious. I hit *Send* and waited.

Auntie Akamai glanced at the text and let out a chuckle. "He's going to a party dressed like a sumo wrestler," she told Stella while texting me back.

I agree. We need to be careful. No more texts.

* * *

The sun was going down as we arrived at the Aloha Lagoon Resort and Stella found parking. As we walked across the street, Stella went between Auntie Akamai and me and linked arms.

Was it just me, or was she making an effort to keep Auntie Akamai and me apart? She couldn't be with both of us all night… I had to give her the slip. It shouldn't be too hard. Stella couldn't expect me to hang out with ladies forty years older than myself at a wedding of people my age. I needed to find someone to attach to…

Auntie Akamai must've read my mind.

"Stella, let's go see Cain and Jennifer," she said, giving Stella a tug to the right.

"Kiki should come too," Stella said, her clamp of an arm pinning me to her side.

"No, no," said Auntie Akamai. "She should go greet the bride and groom. She actually has an invitation as a guest." She turned to face us and physically pried Stella off me like she was a starfish and I was a rock. Auntie Akamai gave me a gentle push away and a meaningful look.

You don't have to give me a chance to escape twice.

I hurried off to look for the bride and groom.

At one end of the open field where hula performances usually took place, there were chairs set up in rows, facing away from me toward a dais, where presumably the nuptials would occur. The opposite end had a display, and the two sides of the open area were a bar and, across from it, the food. Standup tables dotted the open area.

"Kiki," called out a familiar voice, and I turned to see Analise. She had on a simple white T-shirt with *ALL THAT* painted in block letters on it. She was, of course, zombified, but it looked like a quickie job from one of the on-site makeup artists.

"Hi Analise," I said, studying her shirt.

She glanced down to see what I was staring at. "Oh, yeah," she laughed. Then she beckoned a man to her and grabbed his hand when he got close enough. He was also wearing a plain white T-shirt, but an empty chip bag was stapled to it in the center of his chest.

Analise pulled him to her left side and pointed to herself, paused, and then pointed at the man. "Get it now?" She gave the man a withering look. "You have to stay here or we both look stupid, Grayson."

I looked them over in the order she directed. "All that…and a bag of chips!" I laughed. "Yes, I get it now. Very clever."

She took a step closer to me. "You look amazing! Your makeup! Did you do that yourself?"

I shook my head. "No, the creepy neighbor did it for us. Oh," I said and dug around in my bag for the envelope and a pen. "The card. You want to sign it?"

"Oh, of course, thanks," she said and used the guy's back as a desk to sign her name. "I'll pay you back for half that gift card." When she came back around the side of her portable chip bag-slash-desk, she pointed at him. "This is Grayson. Grayson, Kiki."

Still mute, he nodded and shook my hand. *I guess chip bags don't speak?*

"I'm going to go hit the open bar," Analise said. "What are you up to?"

"I'm starving." I gestured toward the catering tables. "I should eat before I drink."

"Okay, I'll see you later," Analise called over her shoulder as she and Grayson left for the bar.

I hadn't even decided which way to walk when a young man dressed as a zombie waiter came by with a tray of appetizers. I recognized the fancied-up amputated finger cookies from the World Fusion Café and, on second look, realized the zombie waiter was Noah.

I stepped in front of him. "Noah, hey." I looked down at the tray like I was trying to decide on which nail art pattern for my next manicure.

"Hey, Kiki," Noah muttered. "I'm working."

"I can see that," I said, reaching for a finger and then pretending to hesitate on my choice. "So, did your grandma Stella do your makeup?" I chose a finger cookie with a bloodred almond slice nail with evil yellow eyes and vampire fangs.

Noah was staring at me. "No. I did it myself."

"Really? Wow, you're good!" I inspected his work. "For real, you could get paid to do it."

He nodded and cleared his throat. "I'd like to go to art school next year." He raised the tray slightly. "I did the fingernails, too. I inherited the artist genes."

"Not pineapple ones?" I asked him.

He blushed under all that gray makeup.

I leaned in. "I thought I didn't have a choice, Noah. But you can make your own choices, be your own person."

His brows furrowed and his jaw tightened. "Not in my family."

I put my free hand on his arm. "Yes, even in your family." To cover for my touching the waiter (my mother would have fainted at the sight), I grabbed another finger cookie. I used it to tap my temple then turned away.

Noah clearly wasn't interested in being the sole heir for the pineapple plantation, not that he had much choice in the matter of his birth.

When I turned, I saw the catering table and one very angry-looking zombie staring me down.

Jennifer.

I wasn't ready to deal with her yet. Luckily, an announcement was made to please find a seat for the ceremony to begin. The groom, Tim, and his best…zombie stood on a dais with a zombied minister. Or, more likely, a justice of the peace. I giggled. *A justice of the undead?*

I found a seat, and to my surprise, Auntie Akamai slid onto the chair next to me.

"I finally gave her the slip when they asked her to decorate someone," she said. Then she tipped her head. "I wonder if decorate is the right term. It's more like undecorate."

"I spoke to Noah for a moment," I told her. "He is apparently quite the artist too—he did his own makeup. He commented it was in his genes."

Auntie Akamai took my hand and squeezed it. "I'm sorry I didn't mention Stella's daughter was Noah's mom. I don't know what I was thinking, assuming you knew."

I nodded. "I know you weren't hiding it, but I do think it makes a difference." I lowered my voice to a whisper because the wedding march started. "I just don't know how yet."

We stood and turned to the middle aisle. Shannon was walking arm-in-arm with her undead dad, and she was clutching dead flowers in her hands. Her dress was beautiful, in a strange way—I thought it was probably a new, stunning gown at some point in history, but now it was grayed and torn. Dried flowers sprouted from the slits and trailed down the skirt.

"That is oddly beautiful," Auntie Akamai whispered.

I nodded my agreement, and after the pair reached the dais and the bride's father passed her off to her groom, we sat.

I didn't listen much to the words. I was daydreaming instead about a wedding of my own someday. It would certainly be different than this one—I would want sun and sea and sand… I smiled to myself when I realized who was all those things to me. Dex.

The crowd chuckled, startling me out of my daydream and back into the nightmarish Hallo-wedding. I'd missed a joke or something. I leaned over to Auntie Akamai and asked what everyone laughed about.

"The minister asked us to recognize Shannon and Tim, the newly*deads*." She smiled. "Everything is so clever."

The couple kissed, the music started—"The Monster Mash"—and the couple pranced back down the aisle, Shannon waving her dead flower bouquet in the air. The same voice that urged us into the seating now directed us to the lawn behind the seating for the reception.

Auntie Akamai and I made our way out of the seating and into the open area. We headed for the bar tables first and saw a familiar face serving up the wine.

"Akamai, Kiki! I thought that was you!" Margaux waved to us. Half her head was messed up, and there was a "gaping wound" on her abdomen. "Pretty gross, huh?"

"That is…impressive," said Auntie Akamai. "This is certainly a different kind of wedding, isn't it?"

"I think it's fun!" Margaux said. "Red or white?"

"White," Auntie Akamai and I said in unison.

As we were waiting, Auntie Akamai gave me a look from the corner of her eye. "So. Margaux. Stella told me about the secret."

Margaux's steady pour wavered enough to splash out of the glass. "I'm not sure what you mean," she said before handing the glass to me. "We can talk later, Akamai. There's a line forming." And she turned away to the next zombie in line.

CHAPTER THIRTY-TWO

We turned away and began walking.

"Are you going to explain?" I asked Auntie Akamai.

"I was bluffing," she explained. "I know there's something I haven't figured out and it's connected somehow to the attempts on Oliana's life. But I can't work it out."

"Margaux's response makes me think she does know something, don't you think?" I asked.

Auntie Akamai nodded. "Yes, or she had a line of people to serve."

"But her hand shook," I pointed out. We stopped and faced each other.

"I saw that too," Auntie Akamai said.

"You know," I said, "I think you need to sit down with Oliana. She has to have an idea what is going on. What secret is being kept."

Auntie Akamai frowned. "I agree. If she insists on keeping it, it might end up killing her. Literally." She pulled out her phone. "I'll send her a text. She's still in the hospital, but she texted me earlier, so I know she has her phone."

I looked around. "I should probably give the happy couple our well-wishes."

It wasn't hard to find Shannon and Tim, the happy undead bride and groom. As soon as I started looking, they were making their rounds, holding hands and smiling ear to mangled ear.

"Kiki!" Shannon squealed. "Thank you so much for coming! You look great!"

"Oh, thank you for inviting me!" I said back. "This is a lot of fun. And your dress is gorgeous." I set my wine on the table next to me and dug around in my messenger bag. "Analise and I went in together," I said, handing her the card.

"Oh, you didn't have to," she said, accepting the card. "I didn't invite you to make sure we got gifts!"

The three of us chuckled awkwardly.

"But thank you," Tim said. "We appreciate it."

"Oh, yes, of course," said Shannon. "We do." She pointed to my outfit. "You said Nancy Drew, right? I can totally see it."

I slapped my forehead. "I totally forgot my props!" I pulled out the flashlight and magnifying glass and held them up.

"Cute!" she said. "I used to love Nancy Drew. Do you read mysteries?"

I smiled. "Not much. But I do solve them." I winked and held the magnifying glass up to my eye and squinted through it at them as they laughed.

If only they knew.

Shannon and Tim headed off to greet other guests. I slipped the flashlight back into my bag and picked up my wine again. My phone buzzed with a text from Auntie Akamai.

Oliana asked me to come talk to her at the hospital. Taking Stella's car. Be back soon.

I acknowledged it with a thumbs-up then wandered to the catering spread and picked a few sushi rolls made to look like eyeballs and some fruits carved into various things. I picked some guava carved into an anatomically correct heart, dragon fruit bones and skulls, and banana slices made to look like little brains. The "eyeballs" were a hard pass—the catering card said they were longan, but they honestly didn't look like anything I'd care to ingest.

I moved down the table, looking over the other offerings. I saw celery witch brooms, just like Auntie Akamai's, and piles of the mummy-wrapped pigs in a blanket.

"So original," I muttered.

"We did our best on the short notice," said Cain Harris from the other side of the table. "And by the way, Akamai suggested these finger foods."

If he wasn't a forty-something-year-old man, I'd swear I saw him roll his eyes. Looked like his wife was rubbing off on him.

"I didn't know your first wife was Stella Keawe's daughter," I said. "I had no idea Stella was your mother-in-law and Noah's grandma."

He sighed. "Why would you, Kiki? You don't know the first thing about us."

"I know some things," I said. "Like Noah wants to be an artist."

Cain looked away. "I know. Trust me, I know."

Jennifer appeared at his side. "Well, hey there, Nancy Drew. Are you interrogating my husband now?"

Cain shot her a look. "Don't start this, not now, Jennifer." He turned to me. "We're working, Kiki. Thank you for bringing the job to us, but please, let us work."

"And stay away from our son," Jennifer added as a parting shot.

* * *

I wandered around, chitchatting with people I knew and looking at the costumes. I got a second wine from a bartender I didn't know and snagged a few more sushi eyes, avoiding Cain and Jennifer. I almost ran into Stella, sitting and painting a late arrival. I quickly turned around and went the other way to check out a large photo display of the happy couple. As I was looking at it, an arm slipped around my shoulders.

"Hey there, Kiki," Analise giggled. "How're you doing?"

I smiled at her. "I'm doing good. Maybe not as good as you are!"

She giggled again and put her face close to mine. "Guess what."

"What?" I asked her.

She leaned even closer but whispered loudly. "I lost my bag of chips."

"Oh?" I looked around, but sure enough, no bag of chips.

"He's over behind a tree getting to know a zombie hula dancer," Analise snorted. "He thinks she's more of 'all that' than I am." She pointed at her shirt.

My mouth dropped open. "Whoa. Is he your boyfriend?"

She laughed and dropped her arm from my shoulders. "Naw. I barely know him. It's no biggy. I think it's funny."

Hilarious.

"Dismembered fingers, ladies," said a voice from behind us.

Analise and I turned around to face Noah.

His face fell. "Oh, it's you guys. I didn't recognize you."

"Oh, come on, *bro*," Analise slurred, reaching for a finger cookie. "How can you not recognize me? *Bro*."

I watched her, confused why she was calling Noah "bro."

Noah seemed to agree it was odd.

"Don't call me bro, Analise." Noah started to turn to leave.

"Oh, come on, lil bro, don't leave." Analise put her hand on his arm, but he pulled away. She followed him as he stormed away with his tray of finger cookies.

What was with that?

I shook my head and turned away and found myself face-to-face with Jennifer.

"I thought I told you to stay away from Noah," she said, getting up in my face.

I took a step back, lifting my hands in front of me in surrender. "He approached me and Analise to offer us cookies. I did not approach him," I said. "In fact, I didn't even speak to him."

Jennifer's eyebrows went down. "Analise spoke to him?"

I frowned back at her. "She didn't say much, but she followed him when he left."

"What'd she say to him?" she asked, taking a step closer to me.

I took a step back. "He had offered us fingers, and then said he hadn't recognized us. She said something like 'how could you not recognize me, bro?'"

"She said…" Jennifer trailed away. "She must know." She whipped her head around, looking for them. "How does she know?"

"Know what?" I asked.

Jennifer shook her head, still craning it around to look for her son. "Never mind."

And she hurried off.

What in the heck was going on?

CHAPTER THIRTY-THREE

I glanced around then pulled out my phone to text Auntie Akamai.

How's it going? I asked her.

Oli has an interesting theory, she responded. *I'm heading back in a few.*

OK, I typed. *I think it's wrapping up here for me anyway.*

Auntie Akamai sent a thumbs-up emoji, and I slipped my phone back into my bag.

When I looked up from doing that, someone running at the edge of the festivities caught my eye. *Who was that?*

I set my empty wineglass on the closest table and jogged in the direction of the running person. "Jogged" might not be the best description, since I was in chunky heels and trying to avoid getting them dirty. That became harder when I got to a row of bushes I would have to push through in order to find whoever I saw running.

Then I heard voices.

I strained to hear them, but they were too low and muffled. The voices were close though.

I crept along the bushes, peering around them and straining to hear. I froze when I heard movement on the other side of the bushes.

"Did you tell him?" one voice said.

"No," said another voice with a whimpering feel to it. "Of course not."

"He can't know!" said the first voice.

I leaned forward and moved my head around, trying to see through the branches, and finally got the owners of the voices into view.

Jennifer, the first voice, spoke again. Her back was to me.

"Analise, do you understand me? He cannot know." Jennifer had a hand raised at Analise. I couldn't tell if there was something in her hand or not.

Analise, backed up against a palm tree, wasn't looking her best. In fact, as I watched, she was slowly sliding down.

"What are you doing?" asked Jennifer, right before Analise doubled over and threw up—probably right on Jennifer's feet. "Oh, you stupid girl!"

Jennifer shoved Analise away from her, and Analise fell like a sack of potatoes. Jennifer cursed and stormed off, away from me. I waited a moment until I could no longer hear her stomping away then slipped through the bushes to Analise, stepping carefully to avoid soiling my Louboutins.

"Analise," I said, shaking her. Her head lolled back and forth. I went down onto my knees and made sure she was breathing then pushed her hair away from her face to pat her cheek, and my hand hit something wet.

Oh, gross.

I pulled the flashlight out of my bag and turned it on and was surprised to see blood trickling down the side of her face. I stared, confused. She was lying on her left side so I was looking at the right side of her face.

Analise moaned and raised a hand to the area that was bleeding.

I grabbed her hand. "Hold on, Analise. Don't touch it. Let me find something to hold on it." I shined my flashlight into my bag and dug around to find something. I found a pack of tissues, but that surely wasn't going to help much.

"Here," said a voice from behind me. "Use this to stop the bleeding."

I startled so badly I dropped the flashlight.

I turned to see Stella holding out a rag. I gasped, then took the rag with a thank you.

"Is she okay?" Stella glanced around. "I saw a figure running and then saw you follow. I wanted to know what you're up to."

"She must've hit the tree pretty hard." I pressed the cloth to Analise's head, causing her to moan.

"How did that happen, Nancy Drew?" scoffed Stella.

I leaned over Analise. "What happened, Analise? Did Jennifer hit you?"

Analise mumbled something.

"Did she hit her head when she fell to the ground?" Stella asked.

I shook my head. "I don't think so. She's on her left side, but the injury is on the right." I felt around on the ground until I found my flashlight then lifted the rag to check the bleeding. It had stopped.

"Should we call 9-1-1?" Stella asked, leaning closer.

"No, I think we can drive her to the hospital. It's already stopping," I said, dabbing the wound again. "I'd hate to have the wedding be *too* memorable."

"Wait," ordered Stella. "Pull the cloth away again."

I did as I was told and leaned to the side a little so she could get closer.

"Kiki…" Stella started laughing. "That's a fake wound."

"*What?*" I stared and dabbed at the wound until I cleaned it completely off her head. "Oh, geesh. But it felt wet…" I poked the side of her head with my finger. Shaking my head, I stood and looked down at Stella, keeping a firm grip on my flashlight.

"Miss Stella, what the heck is going on?" I asked. "I know you know something."

Stella stared at me for a few seconds. "I can't say anything. I promised her."

"Who?" I glanced down at Analise then around us. "Analise? Or Jennifer?"

She shook her head, and in the faint light, it looked like her eyes were filling with tears.

"Oh," I said. "Your daughter."

She nodded, and a few tears spilled out. "She made me promise not to tell before she died."

"What?' I asked, reaching out a hand to her arm. "What can't you tell?"

She frowned through her tears at me. "Do you not understand the point of a promise?"

"But is keeping this promise worth people getting hurt?" I asked. "Celine is dead, and maybe the same person tried to kill Oliana, getting Dex injured, too. Would your daughter have wanted that?"

When she didn't answer, I tried a different tack. "It seems like Margaux knows something about a secret. Is it the same one?" Still silence. "And there was something Jennifer said…"

Stella waved a hand to dismiss my questions. "Let's get this stupid girl up. Who can we call to pick her up?"

I shrugged. "She was here with someone, but it didn't sound like someone who would be helpful. I met her mother once but don't know how to get ahold of her."

"Who is she?" Stella asked, pointing at Analise. "Maybe I know her mother."

"Analise," I said, pointing at the young woman on the ground. "Celine's niece."

Stella's head snapped down to look at her. "Bette's daughter?"

I nodded. "Oh, yeah, that was her name."

Stella was still staring at Analise. "Well, I can't be here, then." She turned to leave.

I grabbed her arm. "Stella, she needs help." Suddenly it hit me what Jennifer was saying to her. "Jennifer was saying Analise couldn't tell a 'him' something, that 'he' couldn't know. Did she mean Noah?"

Stella stopped but didn't turn back.

"What can't Analise tell Noah, Stella?"

Stella pulled her arm from my grip and hurried away.

I watched her go then looked down at Analise. "Girl, what do you know?" I asked her prone form.

She answered with a soft snore.

* * *

After positioning Analise on her side in case she got sick again, I hurried back to the field. Slipping around the photo display, I paused. I had to decide who was the better option for help. The bar or the catering table? Margaux, or Jennifer and Cain Harris?

As luck would have it, I saw someone else near the catering table. I was fairly sure it was Analise's mom. I hurried up to the woman and peered at her.

"Excuse me? Are you Analise's mom?" I asked the woman.

She turned and looked at me. "Yes. Do you know where she is?"

I nodded. "I think she drank too much. She's passed out over in the bushes."

Her mom rolled her eyes. "Okay. Show me."

I led her toward the photo display. "Is she okay? I mean, her state of mind?"

Her mother shook her head. "Something has been bothering her. But I don't know what." She raised a hand to wipe at her face. "Even before my sister died."

I led her off the field and through the bushes to where I had left Analise. "Watch where you step," I told Bette. I stopped in front of the tree.

A painting rag lay crumpled on the ground, but there was no sign of Analise.

CHAPTER THIRTY-FOUR

Bette, Analise's mom, was rightfully freaked out when I told her this was where I'd left Analise.

"Maybe the guy she came with found her and helped her home?" I suggested, training my flashlight beam around the area.

Bette shook her head. "No, I doubt it. She texted me he was being a jerk."

"I shouldn't have left her," I said, staring at the ground where she had been. "But I was going to get help. I laid her on her side in case she got sick…"

Bette took a deep breath. "It's not your fault, Kiki. But we need to find her." She pulled out her phone and clicked on the flashlight, and we began to search.

I discovered quickly that there were only a few feet until the bushes cleared and we entered a parking lot. A chill ran through me when I realized Analise could've easily been put in a car and taken away.

Bette came up next to me at the edge of the parking lot and stopped. We looked at each other.

"We need to call the police," I said to her.

* * *

While Analise's mother called the police, I hurried back through the bushes to see if Analise had somehow made it back out to the field. There had only been a couple minutes between me leaving Analise and finding her mother, so it was unlikely that she came to and walked after me. I ran over to the bar.

"Margaux, have you seen Analise?" I asked. "You know her?"

"Yes, I know Analise." I think she could tell by my tone that I was not playing around. "I haven't seen her in a while, since I denied serving her another drink. Why?"

"She's disappeared. She was sick and passed out in the bushes, and I came out to get help, and when I went back, she was gone." I pointed at the area we had been.

Margaux immediately wiped her hands and came around the edge of the table, leaving it in the hands of the other bartenders. We agreed to meet on the other side of the field and weaved through the partygoers, looking for Analise. When we both emerged on the other side, her face was etched with worry.

Together, we hurried the rest of the way to the catering table.

"Jennifer," Margaux said to the other woman. "You know Analise, Celine's niece? Have you seen her?"

Jennifer looked her right in the eye and lied. "Who?"

"What do you mean, who?" I almost shrieked at her. "I saw you talking to her, calling her by name!"

Margaux looked from me to Jennifer. "Is that true, Jennifer?"

"Of course not," Jennifer said.

"I saw you with her not even ten minutes ago!" I shouted. "Why are you lying?"

Margaux put an arm around my shoulder and steered me away.

"She's lying!" I hissed at Margaux. "*Why is she lying?*"

"I don't know, but making her angry isn't going to help." Margaux marched me away and to the seating for the wedding. She pushed me down into a chair. "Stay here. I'll go grab you a drink."

Oh heck no.

As soon as she had her back turned, I got up and hurried into a large group of partiers. I found the bride and groom in the middle of the group. At least they were having a good time.

I stood awkwardly on the other side of the group and waited. I needed to think.

After seeing Analise talking to Noah, Jennifer said to Analise that *he can't know*. Then Analise was sick. Now she was missing, and Jennifer was claiming to not know her.

Then there was Stella. She promised her dead daughter she would keep a secret. That daughter had been married to Cain and was Noah's birth mother.

There was no way there wasn't a connection there.

It had to be the same secret and must have to do with Noah.

I had to find Noah—but if this secret was being kept from him, he probably wouldn't be of much help with it. But he could help me look for Analise. He obviously knew her.

I peered around the partygoers to the catering table. I didn't see him there, though he had been circulating with food, not standing behind the table each time I saw him.

I did spot Margaux though, and she spotted me. I fought the urge to run as she approached me.

"You scared me, Kiki, disappearing like that!" Margaux frowned at me. "There's already one missing girl!"

"I'm sorry. I hadn't thought about it like that," I said. "I was looking for Analise."

Margaux nodded her chin toward the back of the field. "The police are here now, anyway. You should probably talk to them."

I hurried across the field with her to Analise's mother, who had her arms tightly crossed to keep her tears in.

"Oh, there you are Kiki. They need more details," she said to me.

I led them back to the tree where I had left Analise, pointed out the physical evidence she had left behind (partly so they wouldn't step in it), and explained the rag.

"So, her head wasn't bleeding?" the uniformed officer asked me.

I shook my head. "It was convincing makeup." When the officer looked confused, I pointed in the direction of the wedding. "Everyone here is a zombie for a wedding."

The officer shook his head and made a note on his notepad. "Tourists," he muttered.

"So why did you think she was bleeding?" he asked.

I hesitated a moment then went through all of my interactions with Analise, Jennifer, and Noah.

"And where is Jennifer Harris now?" a second officer asked.

I pointed toward the wedding again. "At the catering table. She denied even knowing Analise, despite me seeing her talk to her. And I haven't seen Noah since Analise was talking to him."

The second officer jogged off in the direction I had pointed at the same time as a third appeared at the tree.

"I found this in that parking lot," she said to the first officer, holding out a gloved hand. It was a necklace.

Analise's mother leaned in to look then clapped a hand to her mouth and began crying.

"Is that Analise's necklace?" I asked her.

She nodded. "She never takes it off," she sobbed.

The first officer pulled out his radio and stepped away. I couldn't hear what he was saying, but by the urgency of his tone, I made a guess he was updating a missing person to a possible kidnapping.

* * *

Unfortunately for the zombie bride and groom, their party came to a pun-intended dead halt. The police gathered all the guests and began questioning them one by one. I was told I was free to go after giving the police my contact information (like they didn't already have it after the past nine months…). I lingered anyway, ignoring the glares coming from the catering table area. The Harrises had some nerve being angry with me when Jennifer lied straight to my face about Analise. I fought the urge to stick my tongue out at the couple.

I did notice Noah was nowhere in sight.

I got a text from Auntie Akamai. *What the heck is going on at the wedding?* she asked. *There are cops everywhere!*

Analise is missing, I said. *Long story, but I think it could be involved with the murder/attempted murder.*

A moment later, my phone rang.

"Can you talk?" asked Auntie Akamai quietly.

"Yes, but this might be easier in person," I said. I looked around. Stella was still in the group of not-yet-released. "Come pick me up. There's somewhere I think we need to go first."

CHAPTER THIRTY-FIVE

I ran through the evening as we drove to Celine's house.

"So Jennifer denied even knowing Analise right after talking to her?" Auntie Akamai said. "This is so bizarre."

"Cain did tell Dex and me that Jennifer was super overprotective of Noah," I pointed out. "And clearly, there is a secret that Analise knows that she isn't supposed to tell Noah."

"So why are we going to Celine's house?" Auntie Akamai asked.

"Because somehow, it has to do with Celine," I said, fidgeting with my messenger bag. I had neglected to remove it before buckling my seat belt, and now the flashlight was poking me in the side. "Remember how upset Noah was about Celine? And Analise is her niece."

Auntie Akamai nodded. "Okay, and what is your theory about the secret?"

I held up my hands. "I'm not sure. Stella is very secretive about her daughter being Noah's biological mother, right? And now she said there is something she promised her daughter before she died. Something her daughter made her promise not to tell."

Auntie Akamai nodded her head. "I think I can fill in a blank for you." She pulled to the side of the street a few houses down from Celine's and turned off the Jeep.

"Oliana," I said. "She told you something."

Auntie Akamai nodded as she unbuckled her seat belt. I did the same and shifted my bag slightly to relieve myself of the poking.

"Oliana thinks Cain might not be Noah's father," she said. "I put it off to her being ornery, but when you consider it with what you just said, she could be right."

"Why does Oliana think that though?" I asked. "Not that it isn't making sense."

Auntie Akamai frowned. "Oliana has always felt Noah didn't look enough like Cain."

If I were being honest, I'd never studied Noah's features—or Cain's—enough to consider. "What do you think? You know them better."

She shook her head. "Hawaiians are often a blend of cultures anyway, especially Japanese and Pacific Islander. I've never dissected the boy's features."

"Who would know the truth?" I asked. "It sounds like Stella may, but in honoring her promise to her daughter, she won't tell. But somehow, Analise must have found out."

"Well, and Jennifer obviously knows something," Auntie Akamai pointed out. She looked down the street at Celine's house. "Why exactly did you want to come here?"

"Just a hunch. Noah was close to Celine, and he was the only person I know who I didn't see after Analise disappeared." I gestured at her house. "If no one is here, then we're good to go."

Auntie Akamai reached for the door opener then dropped her hand and turned back to me. "What would all this have to do with Celine dying? Or someone trying to kill Oliana?"

I pursed my lips. "The only thing that comes to mind is the inheritance he would eventually get from Oliana. But why now is the question."

"Well," said Auntie Akamai. "Let's go see if there are answers."

* * *

Auntie Akamai and I crept through Celine's front gate. It was spring-loaded, so I gently let it close behind me.

The house was dark, but there were occasional flashes of light and snippets of voices around the side of the house. I followed Auntie Akamai down the dark path between Celine's prized shrubbery until she waved me to stop behind a large (probably poisonous) bush. Voices were coming through better now.

"Just tell me, Analise. Tell me what you know!" begged Noah with a sob. "Why won't anyone tell me?"

"I don't know anything, Noah." Analise's voice had a strangled edge to it. "Why do you think I know something about you?"

"You called me bro!" Noah shouted at her then calmed himself. "Are you my sister? Was my mom your mom?"

"No, man. No. Bro is just a, you know, a term for a guy," Analise said.

I peered through the branches of the bush at the pair. Analise was on the ground by her namesake Bougainvillea, and Noah was crouching over her. He looked very twitchy, and I jumped when I saw why Analise sounded so panicked.

Something in Noah's hand glinted in the moonlight.

I looked over at Auntie Akamai, and she nodded. I couldn't see her expression in the dark, but I knew she saw the object too and was worried.

"Why are you doing this, Noah?" Analise asked. "Why did you do any of this?"

"I haven't done anything," Noah said, anger flaring again. "Everyone looks at me funny, talks about me behind my back, gives each other looks… There is something everyone knows about me *except* for me!"

"Have you asked your mom?" Analise asked.

Noah threw up his hands. "She's the worst of all!" His mood shifted again, and he leaned over Analise, pointing the shiny thing away from her. "Why did Miss Celine name *that* bush after me?"

With his arm extended, I could see what he held in his hand. It was a pointy plant clipper. *Very* pointy.

Auntie Akamai leaned out to see what he was pointing at with those clippers. I looked too. It was a smaller flowering Bougainvillea plant I hadn't paid any attention to the other night.

"What?" Analise's voice wavered. "What are you talking about?"

Noah sat back on his heels. "Look, Miss Celine named this one after you, right? 'Cause you're her niece." He pointed at the smaller one. "She told me she named that one after me."

Analise's face scrunched up. "She did?"

"Yes. Does that mean I'm her nephew?" Noah asked.

Analise stared at him. "How…?" She tried to push herself into a more upright position, but he stuck the plant clippers into her face and she froze. "Noah," she said quietly. "Did you hurt Celine?"

He shook his head. "No. No!"

Auntie Akamai suddenly stepped out into the path. "Noah, put down the clippers."

Noah, on his knees, spun around and stood in one fluid motion, holding the clippers in front of him toward Auntie Akamai. "What? *How?*" he said.

"Everyone is looking for Analise. They think she's been kidnapped. We just need to let them know she's okay," Auntie Akamai said calmly, gesturing him to her.

"No. I need answers!" Noah shouted. "I need to know!"

I reached into my bag and felt around for the hefty flashlight, wrapping my fingers around it and holding on.

"And you will, Noah," said Auntie Akamai soothingly. "But not like this. You'll be eighteen soon, right? Perhaps they were waiting until then. But you can ask them. You don't have to hurt Analise to get your answers. You just need to ask."

While she was talking, she made tiny steps toward him. Each tiny step she took, he extended his arm farther toward her.

"You don't think I have?" Noah whined. "I tell my mom I know there is something and that I'm going to ask Celine, that she'll tell me, and next thing I know, she's dead!"

I gasped, and Noah craned to look around Auntie Akamai. I froze and waited.

Auntie Akamai started talking again to cover me. "Wait, you're saying you told Jennifer that you were going to talk to Celine right before Celine died?"

Noah nodded, and tears started to fall from his eyes. "She's dead because I wanted to know."

I started to move around the far side of the bush, moving slowly and hoping his tears would make me invisible.

"Did Jennifer…" Auntie Akamai started to ask but then stopped herself. "What about Oliana? Do you know what happened to her? To her car?"

Noah shook his head. "I heard my mom and Oliana arguing. Then she was in the accident."

"What did they argue about?" Auntie Akamai asked.

I leaned until I could see Analise. She was scootching away on her rear, little by little.

Until she hit a dry branch, which snapped.

Noah spun around and lunged at her, clipper arm extended.

And I jumped out from behind the bush, flashlight in hand, and conked Noah on the head.

CHAPTER THIRTY-SIX

I sat in the back of one police cruiser while Auntie Akamai was being questioned. Noah sat in the back of another, in handcuffs, and Analise was sitting on the curb being checked out by EMTs. Other than some scrapes, Analise would be fine, or at least until her hangover started.

At Auntie Akamai's urging, the police who responded to her 9-1-1 call contacted Detective Ray, who now walked up to the squad car I was in. He opened the door and squatted in front of me.

"No scars this time," he said dryly.

"Not real ones, at least," I said, poking at the fake scar on my face.

"So, tell me," Detective Ray said.

"You don't have your murderer," I said, nodding toward Noah. "He didn't say it outright, but he made it sound like Jennifer killed Celine to keep her from telling Noah something."

"Telling him what?" Detective Ray frowned.

"I don't know for sure, but I think Cain isn't his real father. I'm not sure why that's worth killing someone though." I shook my head. "If I had to guess, I'd say his real father is someone close to Celine. It sounds like he and Celine are related, and that's what Jennifer didn't want him to know."

"If he's not biologically Cain's or Jennifer's son, would he still stand to inherit the pineapple fortune?" Detective Ray asked.

I shrugged. "They raised him as theirs. It shouldn't matter to them. He, on the other hand, is really upset about them keeping something from him. And rightfully so." I held up a hand. "It's possible that Cain didn't know either."

"The question would be who *did* know." Detective Ray stood. "We'll have to ask Jennifer. We have her down at the station about Analise's disappearance, but she doesn't know about this development. We'll figure out her motive soon enough."

"Detective Ray," I called out as he was turning.

He faced me again.

"He turns eighteen soon. Is he going to be okay? Like, legally?" I asked.

Detective Ray raised a shoulder. "I don't know at this point. It depends on what he's done and if whoever he's wronged wants to hold him accountable."

"Maybe call Stella to come be with him," I said. "For two reasons, really. One, she is one person we know is a support to him and related by blood. Plus, I'm pretty sure she knows the truth about his biological father. Maybe she'll tell you, or at least be there to soften the blow… He's hurting," I said, looking back at Noah. "Go easy on him."

* * *

Two days later, a small group of us gathered in Oliana's gold-gilded sitting room to get an update. I sat between Dex and Auntie Akamai on the couch while Oliana Harris and Detective Ray sat in twin chairs. Oliana dismissed a nurse with a disgusted wave of her hand and a mutter no one wanted to decipher. Noah and Analise sat together on a loveseat.

"So," Detective Ray said, looking around the room. "Are there any questions?"

Auntie Akamai and I glanced at each other. The questions we had discussed at home could hardly be discussed in front of some of these people. Like, was Oliana going to disinherit Noah? How did Jennifer find out about Noah's father? And, of course, who *is* Noah's father?

Oliana apparently had no qualms.

"Cain is not Noah's father, correct?" She asked a question, but her manner of speaking made it an imperious statement.

Detective Ray glanced at Noah. "That is correct."

"Who is his father, then?" she asked.

Detective Ray looked her straight in the eye. "That's not something I feel comfortable divulging."

"Why not? It's the reason behind this mess!" Oliana sat forward and glared.

Detective Ray shook his head. "It honestly is none of your business. It's Noah's decision and, of course, his father's."

Even though I was dying from curiosity, Detective Ray was absolutely right—it was not Oliana's business at all. What she chose to do with the intel of Noah not being her biological grandson was her business, but it's all that was. I wanted to applaud Detective Ray for sticking to his guns with the Pineapple Princess.

"And, I might add, it's not the reason behind the mess. A misguided, overprotective, greedy mother is." Detective Ray nodded to Noah.

"But clearly, Celine's family is involved," said Oliana.

"Yes." Noah spoke up for the first time since entering the room. "Celine was my grandmother." He and Analise exchanged grins.

Auntie Akamai leaned closer to me. "Both her sons were married when Noah would have been conceived," she said quietly into my ear.

"And Celine knew all this time?" sputtered Oliana. "We were friends! How could she not tell me?"

"Because it isn't your business, Oliana," said Noah.

Oliana turned purple, and I wondered if we should summon the nurse.

"How dare you address me by my first name!" Oliana spit out.

"Well, you're not actually my grandmother—not that you ever acted like one," Noah said back to her.

Daaaaaang! Dex and I exchanged looks with raised eyebrows. Part of me wanted to clap Noah on the back. The other part of me was horrified.

Auntie Akamai fell into the horrified category. "Noah!" She shook her head at him. "She may not be your blood, but you still need to be respectful."

Noah lowered his head slightly. "I'm sorry, Auntie Akamai." He glanced at Oliana. "I apologize…Auntie Oliana."

Oliana looked deflated. "You can still call me grandmother," she said softly. "You're my only grandchild."

Noah stared at her, and his eyes filled.

Oliana raised a hand. "That doesn't mean you will still inherit the pineapple plantation. But I won't forsake you," she said. "I need to consult with my lawyer, but I would like to pay for your education. Whatever *you'd* like to study, I mean."

The two exchanged shy smiles.

"Thank you," said Noah. "That would be cool."

Dex raised his good arm. "Can I ask a question?"

Detective Ray nodded to him.

"How did Jennifer find out? Did Celine tell her?" Dex asked.

Detective Ray shook his head. "She said she realized about a year ago when helping Noah with a biology project dealing with genetics. Cain's and Noah's blood types didn't line up."

Across the room, Noah nodded. "I figured it meant my biological mother had a different blood type."

Detective Ray agreed. "But Jennifer went to Stella and somehow tricked her into revealing her daughter, Marti's, blood type. When it didn't match Noah's either, Jennifer realized there was a problem."

Everyone around the room nodded their understanding.

"She says she realized there was a special bond between Celine and Noah and became suspicious," Detective Ray continued. "And then when she confronted Celine about their closeness, Celine made a comment that once Noah was eighteen, he had every right to know about his parentage. Celine intended to tell him and her son."

"Jennifer had to stop Celine from telling," said Analise, shaking her head. "My aunt is dead because Jennifer couldn't cope with Noah knowing the truth." She gazed sadly at her newly minted cousin and squeezed his hand. They had both suffered a big loss.

"Was she worried about the inheritance? That him not being a Harris would somehow exclude him *and* her from receiving any?" I asked.

Oliana snorted. "She says no. She said she was afraid of losing him over the deception."

"So she poisoned Celine to keep the truth—and the deception—from Noah?" I asked.

Detective Ray nodded.

"It's all so stupid," Noah muttered. "She's still my mom. My dad is still my dad. This doesn't change the fact that they raised me. They didn't even know!"

"We think," Analise reminded him.

"But what about the car accident?" Dex asked, gesturing from himself to Oliana.

"She realized Celine dying was causing more scrutiny to their family. She had hoped it would look like an allergic reaction and that was that." Detective Ray looked at Oliana. "The digitalis in her system matches your prescription, by the way, so she took some from your bottle at some point. She might have been intending to frame you."

"How did that work though?" Dex asked. "Did everyone eat the digitalis?"

"We realized the digitalis plus her EpiPen would have caused her heart attack," Auntie Akamai said, gesturing at Oliana at *we*. "For the rest of us, we might feel a little woozy if we tasted her food, but one bite wouldn't have had a big enough affect to notice something was off."

Oliana frowned. "But why kill me? The stolen prescription?"

Detective Ray shrugged. "She said she thought maybe if you didn't know and died without knowing the truth, no one would ever know." He looked at me. "That is where she admitted the inheritance was a motivator. But it was inheritance for him, not her, that she was worried about." He shrugged. "Or so she says."

"I wonder why she wasn't worried about Grandma Stella," Noah said. "I'm glad she didn't try to hurt her too, but I don't know why."

Auntie Akamai smiled. "Stella is a wonderful actress. She must've convinced her that she didn't know anything."

"Or she didn't," I added. "She said she knew her daughter had a secret. She never said she actually *knew* the secret. And honestly"—I cringed as I continued—"if I knew my mother was a huge gossip, I wouldn't have told her either. Her gossiping might have benefited her this time!"

Auntie Akamai laughed. "You might be right."

* * *

Auntie Akamai stayed behind to keep Oliana company while Detective Ray, Dex, Noah, Analise, and I made our way out. We said our goodbyes by our vehicles, and then Dex and I climbed into the Jeep.

I got to drive, of course, which made Dex fussy, but he stopped when he saw a rubber duckie I had snuck onto the dashboard after he got out.

Dex laughed when he picked up the little yellow duck with bandages around its head. "Cute, Kiki. Real cute."

"Laughter is the best medicine, Dex, and you need to heal up quickly if we're still going to New York for Thanksgiving," I said.

"Definitely going," Dex said. "I can't wait. We have to find pet sitters though."

Back at his house, they were preparing for the homecoming of the Great Dane. Dex's mother, in a moment of weakness or perhaps sympathy for his broken arm, agreed to let Scooby move in. Perhaps she was preparing for her son to move out, and thought this might be a good first step.

At Auntie Akamai's house, Paulie and Doyle were tolerating each other. Paulie was still suspicious, while Doyle didn't seem to care either way. Auntie Akamai was thrilled with the new tenant, which probably didn't help Paulie's acceptance of him. We were holding hopes that perhaps someday the two animals would be friends, though images of Sylvester and Tweety weren't far from our minds.

Not far from my mind either was being able to show Dex around New York City, where he had never been. He looked forward to seeing my parents again, or at least said he did. It was only a few short weeks away, and I couldn't wait…but in the meantime, diving adventures beckoned.

ABOUT THE AUTHOR

Rosalie Spielman enjoys moving in order to clean out her closets. After meeting her husband when they were both in the Army, they moved eleven times in twenty-four years, to multiple states and three countries. Somewhere along the way, Rosalie discovered that she could make other people laugh with her writing. She finds joy in giving people a humorous escape from the real world. Her cozy mystery novels are set in locales that have chickens, such as rural Idaho and sunny Kauai.

Rosalie is an active member of Sisters in Crime and is represented by Dawn Dowdle of the Blue Ridge Literary Agency. She currently lives in Maryland with her husband and four creatures—two teens and two fur babies.

To learn more about Rosalie Spielman, visit her online at:
www.rosalie-spielman-author.com

Visit
aloha lagoon

Made in United States
Troutdale, OR
02/09/2024

17542069R00133